Mystery Stories for Boys

Forbidden Cargoes

Mystery Stories for Boys

Forbidden Cargoes

By
ROY J. SNELL

WILDSIDE PRESS

Forbidden Cargoes

CONTENTS

Forbidden Cargoes

CHAPTER I

A STRANGE MESSAGE

In a plain board shack with a palm thatched roof which had the Caribbean Sea at its front and the Central American jungle at its back, a slim, stooping sort of boy, with eyes that gleamed out of the dark corners exactly like a tiger's, paced back and forth the length of a long, low room. His every motion suggested a jaguar's stealth.

It was Panther Eye, a boy who was endowed with a cat's ability to see in the dark, and who spent much of his young life in India and other tropical lands. He also found himself quite at home in Central America. Nevertheless, at this moment he was in deep trouble.

The palm thatched shack boasted but one

room. As the boy paced the mahogany floor of this room he passed a desk of roughly hewn rosewood. A small steel safe stood in one corner, the door slightly ajar. Before it on the floor lay a litter of papers, a few bundles of letters and a sizeable roll of currency. The boy paused to consider this litter.

" It was the map they wanted," he told himself. " Easy enough to see that. They didn't even look at the money, nearly a thousand dollars. The map! They knew we could do nothing without the map. The dirty dogs! If only Johnny Thompson were here! " Again he paced the floor.

What was to be done? His thoughts were in a tangle. The thieves who had broken into the safe were now well away in the jungle. There was no time to be lost. He'd catch them, he was sure of that. A jaguar couldn't escape him, much less a man. Yet the map might be destroyed. Without it nothing could be accomplished. Thousands were at stake, the treasure of a lifetime. And some one dearer to Pant than life itself was scheduled to lose. All day in that stuffy office he had waited for Johnny. Now evening was near.

" If only Johnny would come! " he repeated.

Had he but known it, his good pal, Johnny Thompson, was some three hundred miles away. What was more, he was behind iron bars in a stout stone jail. But this Pant could not know, so he continued to pace the floor.

As the first long shadow of a palm darkened the window he suddenly sprang into action. Throwing up the lid of a rough chest, he tossed out a miscellaneous assortment of articles, some small oilcloth wrapped packages, a black box, some fibre trays, a few articles of clothing and a curious instrument of iron. These he packed carefully in a kit bag, then closed the chest.

Seating himself at the desk in the corner, he began pecking at a small portable typewriter. He destroyed four half written sheets before he did one to suit him. The following is what appeared on the one he at last weighted down upon the desk:

/9*::6

5*3 ;@0 8$ —9:3 5*3 $0@:8@4%$ *@'3 85 8 @; —98:— 8:59 5*3 /7:—#3 @!534 85 8 28## —35 85 :3'34 !3@4 #99= 975 !94 @ $0@:- 8@4% :@;3% %8@(*3 8$ @ %3'8# :3'34 547$5 :94 '3#83'3 *8; !94 @ ;9;3:5

—99% #7?—

0@:5

"There!" he sighed as he turned from the desk. "If Johnny Thompson doesn't make that out right away he won't be coming up to my expectations. And if any of these blacks and browns and whites that infest this waterfront can read it, I take off my hat to 'em."

Turning about, he slung the strap of his kit bag across his shoulder and leaving the cabin, disappeared into the gathering night and the jungle.

Some hours later he might have been found crouching close to the side of a bamboo hut at the heart of the jungle.

His hands trembled as he unwrapped a water-proof package. They trembled still more as he poured a gray powder from the package to a narrow V shaped piece of iron. A little of the powder was spilled over the side and, sinking into the deep bed of tropical moss, was lost forever.

" Won't do," he told himself, stiffening his shoulders. " I've got to get hold of myself. If I don't keep cool I'll make a mess of it and like as not get caught in the bargain.

" Caught by those Spaniards in the heart of the jungle!" He shuddered at the thought. " Caught. And what then?" He dared not think.

" No!" His resolve was strong. " They shall not get me, and I shall succeed. I must!" His face grew tense.

At that he went ahead with his task. Having spread the gray powder evenly along the iron trough, he ran a small black fuse half through it, then gave the fuse five turns about it. When he had finished, the lower end of the fuse hung some six inches below the trough.

" There! " he sighed.

A half hour later found him still crouching at the back of that cabin. This shelter, for it was little more, was of the sort common to the Central American jungle. In its construction not a board and not a single nail was used. A number of cohune nut palms had been felled. Their great fronds had been stripped. The fibre stripped from the stems had been piled in a heap, the stems themselves in another heap. Crotched mahogany limbs were fastened together with tie-tie vines. This made a frame. Rafters were added. The bamboo leaf fibre had been laid carefully in tiers over the rafters. This made a perfect roof. After that the ten foot stems of a great number of leaves were fastened side by side in a perpendicular position to form walls. When this was completed the house was ready to be oc-cupied.

The cracks between the upright bamboo stems forming the walls were wide. A faint light shone through these cracks, and through them the boy could see all that went on with-in. All this interested him, but he was filled with a fever of impatience. He had come to act, not to listen.

Two dark-faced Spaniards sat in the center of the room. Two black bushmen lay sprawled upon the dirt floor. Before them, suspended upon a bamboo frame, was a map. The map, some four feet across, showed cer-tain boundary lines, creeks and rivers. There were spots that had been done in blue. Still others were crisscrossed by pen lines, while larger portions were left white. The figure of one Spaniard hid part of the map.

"Ah!" The boy breathed an inaudible sigh of relief as the man moved, allowing a full view of the map. "Now, if only I can do it!"

With the greatest care, he thrust the triangle of steel upon which the powder rested through a crack. Next he adjusted a small black box before the crack, but lower down. Then, with a hand that still trembled slightly in spite of his efforts at self control, he drew a sulphur match across a dry bit of wood.

The sulphur fumes rose and floated through the cracks. At the same time there came the faint sput-sput-sput of a burning fuse. One of the Spaniards arose and sniffed the air. He spoke a word to a companion. They turned half about. And still the fuse burned. Shorter and shorter it became, closer and closer to the powder.

The boy's heart was in his throat. Was the whole affair to be spoiled by a whiff of sulphur or a fuse that burned too long?

"If they rise, if they block the view," he thought, "then all will be—"

But no, they settled back. The whiff of sulphur had passed. But what was this? A black man jumped. Had the smell of burnt

powder reached him? Had the sput-sput of
the fuse reached his sensitive ear?

Whatever it was, it came too late. Of a
sudden there sounded out a loud boom, and
at once, for a fraction of a second, the whole
place, cabin, bamboo trees, and the surround-
ing jungle was lighted as with a moment's return of the sun. Then came sudden and
complete darkness.

Within was noise and confusion. A bushman had overturned the candle. It had gone
out. In fright and rage at an unknown phenomenon, an unseen enemy, the men fought
their way to the door, then out into the night.
Before this happened, however, the boy, hugging his precious black box under his arm,
had lost himself in the jungle.

As we have said, this boy had lived much in
the tropics. The Central American jungle
was not new to him. Deep secrets of these
wilds had come to him by day and by night.

With the startled cries of Spaniards and
bushmen ringing in his ears, he made his way

swiftly, silently down a narrow deer path to a spot where he had hidden his canvas bound kit bag.

Thrusting his black box deep within the bundle, still without a light, he made his way swiftly forward until the shouts died away in the distance.

" If only it is a success! " he thought with a sigh as he paused to adjust his pack.

Coming at last to a narrow stream he cast a few darting glances about him. The jungle here was new to him, yet the bubbling stream, the moss on the tree trunks, the tossing leaves far above him, told him all he needed to know.

Turning sharply to the right, he followed a narrow trail up the winding bank of the stream.

He had been traveling steadily up this stream for more than three hours when he came upon a place where the stream was a roaring young cataract, tumbling down a series of little falls. This was the thing he had expected. He was sleepy. The night was far spent. In his pack was a mosquito bar canopy and a light, strong hammock, woven from linen thread. With these he could quickly build a safe wilderness home. In the low swamp land, where malaria and mosquitoes lurked, he did not dare to camp.

There were wild creatures in all this jungle; crocodiles, droves of wild pigs, great boa constrictors and golden coated jaguars. For this boy all these held little terror. But the swamps were not for him. The higher slopes of the narrow peninsula offered fresher air, and cooling breezes that lull one to sleep.

" Sleep," he whispered to himself, " and after that a dark place."

At that moment the moonlight, falling through an ·open space among the trees and spreading a yellow gleam upon the trail, showed him that which brought him up short. In a damp spot at the base of a rock were footprints, the marks of a slim foot clad in sandals, and stranger than this in so wild a spot, the marks of a leather shoe.

"Huh!" He stood for a moment in perplexity.

One who knows the jungle is seldom surprised at what he finds there. Pant was surprised. This portion of the jungle was new to him. "Twenty miles from the coast," he murmured. "How strange!"

More was to follow. He had not gone a hundred yards farther before he came upon a well-beaten road. A little beyond this spot, in the midst of a broad clearing, half hidden by stately royal palms, gleaming white in the moonlight, was a long, low stone house which in this land might almost pass for a mansion.

Pausing, he stood there in the moonlight, staring and irresolute. It had all come to him in a flash.

"The last of the Dons," he said to himself. Something akin to awe crept into his tone. "I had forgotten."

"But what now?" he asked himself a moment later. "The jungle or this?"

In the end he chose the castle before him.

" Might be a dark place up there somewhere, an abandoned cellar perhaps," was his final comment.

Having chosen a secluded spot at the side of the trail where he might hang his hammock and spread his canopy to sleep the rest of the night through, he went quickly to rest.

" I have heard that they are friendly, and honorable Spaniards. There are such, plenty of them. I'll risk it. I—"

At that, with the breeze swaying his hammock, he fell asleep.

The sun was sending its first yellow gleams among the palms when he awoke. For a time, with the damp sweet odor of morning in his nostrils, he lay there thinking.

A strange mission had brought him into the jungle. This strange boy had grown up with little or no knowledge of blood relations. His father and mother were but a dim, indistinct memory. They had passed from his life; he did not know exactly how. No cozy home fireside had gleamed for him. He had gone

out into the world with an unanswered longing for some one whom he might think of as
a kinsman. Bravely he had fought his way
through alone. When Johnny Thompson
came into his life and remained there to become his inseparable pal, life had been more
joyous. Yet ever there remained a haunting
dream that somehow, somewhere in his wild
wanderings he would come upon one who
bore his name, who could give him the tradi-
tions of a family and of a past.

Strangely enough, it had been at the edge
of the Central American jungle that he came
upon this person of his dreams. While walking upon the coral beach he had met a stately,
white-haired old man who had the military
bearing of a colonel.

In this old man he had found a friend. Little enough was left of the fortunes which from
time to time had come to the venerable south-
erner. But such as he had he shared unspar-
ingly with the young stranger who had come
so recently from the land of his birth; for

Colonel Longstreet, as the patriarch styled himself, though now for more than sixty years a resident of Central America, had fought valliantly for a lost cause when the Gray stood embattled against the Blue in that long and terrible struggle, the Civil War.

Broken hearted because of the outcome of the war, he had left his native state of Virginia and had come to Central America. His life had been further embittered by the early death of his wife. His only child, a boy of ten, had been sent back to Virginia while he struggled on, wresting a fortune from the jungle.

Life in Central America is one gamble after another. Longstreet had played in every game. He had always won, in the end to lose again. Fortunes in sugar, bananas and mahogany had been his. Sudden drops in prices, a revolution, the dread Panama disease, had cost him all of these. Now he was playing a last, lone card. Influential friends were endeavoring to secure for him a concession for gathering chicle on broad tracts of Government land.

This was the state of affairs when Pant had made his acquaintance. Hardly had their acquaintance ripened into deep friendship when they made the sudden and startling discovery that Pant was the son of the boy who had been sent back by Colonel Longstreet to Virginia, that Colonel Longstreet was none other than Pant's grandfather. From that time forth the strange boy, who had longed for so many lonely years for one of kin, became the old man's devoted slave.

There was need enough at the present time for such devotion.

Fortune had seemed to smile at last. Through the influence of his friends, a concession from the British Government for gathering chicle had come from England to Colonel Longstreet.

" Chicle, as you may know," the old man had smiled, as he told Pant of it, " is the basis of all good chewing gum. Were it not for the great American game of chewing it wouldn't be worth a red cent. As it is, with one company importing two million dollars worth a year and other smaller companies competing and yelling for more, there's a fortune in it. There is a net profit of twenty-five cents a pound on chicle. With proper working, our tract should yield between twenty-five and fifty thousand pounds a year."

With the writings of agreement had come a map showing the exact boundaries of the Government tract they had leased. To the right and above this tract was shown on the map the holdings of a powerful American organization. To the left were tracts leased by an unprincipled Spaniard named Diaz.

Two days after news of the fortunate concession had gone about the little city, Diaz had appeared in the Colonel's small office. He offered a ridiculously low price for the concession. His offer was rejected. He was told that the owner meant to work the concession. He shrugged his shoulders and said:

" No get the men."

The old man had straightened to his full height as he informed the Spaniard that he had men who could be depended upon to go anywhere, to do anything. They had worked with him and knew the honor that lay behind the Longstreet name.

Diaz had begged, entreated, stormed, threatened, then in a rage had left the office.

Two days had passed. On the third day Pant had come to the office only to find the safe looted, the map gone.

" What can we do? " he asked. " We know Diaz has it, but we can't prove it."

" We cannot," the old Colonel had agreed. " Nor is there a chance of getting another before it is too late. The bleeding season for chicle begins with the first rainfall. To begin without a map is to court disaster. With a big and jealous American company on one side of us and a crooked Spaniard on the other, we are between the rocks and the tide. We are sure to encroach upon one or the other. And if we do, it will take all we have to fight their claims. It looks like defeat." He had cupped his hands and had stared gloomily at the sea.

"Wait," Pant had said. " Johnny Thompson will help us out. Give us a little time. We'll find the map. Leave it to us."

Johnny Thompson, as you already know, could not help. He was not there. Two days before he had gone up the Stann Creek Railway. He had not returned. He was in jail. Pant had been obliged to go it alone. "And now in this short time," he told himself, " I have located the map here in the heart of the jungle. No, I haven't got it. That couldn't be done without bloodshed. But I have its equivalent, I hope.

" A dark place! " he exclaimed. " I must find a spot that is absolutely dark."

As he sprang from his hammock he paused to listen. Some one was singing. In a clear girlish voice there came the words of a quaint old Spanish song.

As he parted the branches he saw a plump

Spanish girl, with a round face and sober brown eyes, tripping barefoot down the path. Balanced on her head was a large stone jar.

" Going for the morning water," the boy told himself. " How like those old Bible pictures it all is! "

Twenty minutes later he found himself within the white walls of that ancient and mysterious castle, which had a few hours before loomed so wonderfully out of the night.

CHAPTER II

AN UNDERGROUND SEA

Pant sat in a kitchen so broad and long that it reminded him of a picture he had seen in an illustrated copy of Ivanhoe. The table, on which rested his steaming cup of home grown, home roasted coffee, was a massive hand-hewn affair. On the top, a single slab of mahogany six feet wide and four inches thick, axe marks were yet to be seen.

As his glance took in the room his heart swelled with admiration. There was no stove. A great fireplace was there in its stead. Pots and pans of iron, and of copper and black tin, hung from the rafters.

"Like Longfellow's ancient home," he told himself. "Only this is to-day. The last of the Dons!" he repeated in a tone of reverence.

One thing puzzled him. Every article in the

room, save two, belonged to yesterday—a purple coat hanging in a corner and a boy's cap beside it—were distinctly of to-day and American made.

"They can't belong to the young girl," he told himself. "Nor to her grandmother."

The bent and aged woman who must be the young Spanish girl's grandmother was at that moment offering him his second cup of coffee.

His thoughts were cut short by the answer to his problem. A tall, fair-haired American boy, apparently in his early teens, parted the heavy homespun curtains at the back of the room and started towards the table.

Seeing Pant, he halted in surprise.

"Pardon me," said Pant, springing to his feet. "Perhaps I intrude. I had supposed that this house belonged to these good Spanish people. Apparently it is your home instead."

"No." The strange boy's smile was frank, disarming. "You were right the first time. Like you, I am an intruder. But you are from America," he added quickly. "How perfectly grand! Won't you please stay for a second cup, and to talk to me a little of our homeland?"

Pant stayed. They ended by talking little of the homeland. In their strange surroundings they found a fascinating subject of conversation.

"Yes," said the boy at last, who gave his name as Kirk Munson, "they are truly the last of the Dons. Once a rich and noble family.

"And do you know"—his lips moved close, he spoke almost in a whisper, "there is a tale, perhaps only a legend, a story of a beaten silver box filled with priceless pearls taken from the Pacific when that great ocean was young. The silver box, so the story goes, was hidden away by the first Don of this family to keep it from the buccaneers, hidden and lost from sight of human eyes, perhaps forever.

"There are all sorts of caves and things like that about here," he went on. "It's all very mysterious and—and sort of bewitch-ing."

" Caves?" said Pant, awaking to his most urgent need. " Are they near? Do you sup-pose they are quite dark?"

" I am told," Kirk's voice was low again, " that there is a very great one not four miles back in the bush, and dark. It is said you are no more than inside it before you are fairly immersed in darkness."

" The very place!" exclaimed Pant. " I must go there at once."

" Must you?" Kirk's voice was full of sur-prise.

This changed at once to entreaty. " Won't you please let me go along? No one who lives here will take me. I have a servant, a huge Carib, a very giant of a man who will be our bodyguard."

" That's all right," said Pant, rising. " Be glad for the company. But why do those who live here refuse to enter the cave?"

" Haunted." The other boy's tone was impressive. " They say the cave is haunted by the ghosts of more than a thousand Maya Indians who are supposed to have fled there from their enemies and to have perished centuries ago."

" One wouldn't care to come upon their bones in such a place."

Kirk shuddered.

" Nevertheless, shall we go? " said Pant.

Kirk nodded.

" All right. We had better go up in the cool of late afternoon. The jungle air will not be so oppressive. We can return by the light of the moon."

Late that afternoon, after a day of rest, Pant found himself on the broad veranda of the house. Here he unbound his pack. From it he took three light fibre trays, a package of powders, two flashlights, extra batteries for the lights, and his small black box. All these, together with a quantity of matches, he bound carefully in waterproof oiled cloth. He was then ready for the journey to the cave.

As he sat for a time, waiting for his new found friend, his mind was rife with speculations. How had this strange American boy come here so far from the seaboard? How did he come to be in Central America at all?

The Spanish people were strange, too. He had heard of them, the last of the Dons. Fragments of their history had drifted to him from afar. They were the direct descendants of a proud Spanish family. Two centuries before the family had grown immensely rich, so the story ran. How had they come by their wealth? Where had it gone? These were questions no one seemed prepared to answer. Enough. They were rich no longer. For all that, they appeared to live very comfortably off the land.

" So there is a story, probably only a legend, telling of a box of beaten silver filled with pearls," he thought. " I must know more of that."

He found himself far more interested in the story of that large band of Maya Indians who had perished in the cave. " The thing must have happened long ago," he told himself.

" They did not enter the cave empty handed. When people flee they take some treasures with them. Should one come upon their bones he would be sure to find priceless curios there, beaten gold, hand cut stones and copper knives of long ago."

Yes, he was interested in this a little, but most of all he was concerned with his own business within some dark corner of the cave.

" Wish he'd come," he thought impatiently, " wish—"

At that moment the hugest black man he had ever seen, bearing in one hand a rifle that was a veritable cannon and in the other a basket, rounded the corner of the house. He was closely followed by the American boy.

In a loose flannel blouse, corduroy knickers and high stout boots, Kirk looked quite fit and capable.

" Ready for any adventure," was Pant's mental comment.

"I hope I didn't tire you waiting," Kirk smiled at him. "The Spanish mother put up a bit of lunch for us—casaba bread, home made cheese, butter and wild honey. She insisted; so did Ramoncita. They are dears."

"Real sports, I'd say," Pant assented heartily. He could scarcely remember a time when the very mention of such strange and tasty food did not whet his appetite.

"Ramoncita?" he said after a moment. "Is that the girl with round cheeks and big dark eyes?"

"Yes. Ramoncita Salazar. Musical name, isn't it? The real Spanish people of the highest class are wonderfully attune to all things artistic and beautiful. But we must be off. This black man will go along to help carry our stuff."

The trail they followed was steep and rocky. It was not much of a trail. In places the bushes hung over it so thick and low that they were obliged to all but creep on hands and knees; again it was so smooth and steep that only by clinging to low growing shrubs could they go forward.

For all that, there was something of a trail. Here and there were suggestions of an ancient, permanently cut way. In three places Pant found his feet firmly planted upon steps which had been cut from the solid rock.

"Stands to reason," he said as he perched himself upon the topmost steps of the last flight, "that these were built by natives long ago. See how nature has chipped and worn the edges away."

"Probably done by the Maya Indians centuries ago," said Kirk, dropping upon a soft bed of moss and fanning himself with a broad leaf pulled from a palm. "Everything of importance that is told of the Maya Indians happened long ago. There are a few of them back in the hills now. They do not count any more. A nation that was once rich and in a way powerful, that had a civilization rivaling any to be found in the world five centuries ago, has dwindled to a handful of vagabonds of the jungle. It is sad." He cupped his chin in his hands and, as if seeing the palaces and temples of that lost civilization, sat staring at the jungle. "It is said," he went on at last, "that the cave we are about to visit was the last hiding place of the smartest and wisest of the Mayas."

"Fleeing from the Spaniards?" asked Pant.

"No. The Spaniards have many atrocities justly charged against them. But the great Maya civilization was destroyed by fierce, war-like tribes from the North before the prow of the white man's boat touched Central America's coral strands.

"The last of the Mayas are said to have fled to this cave and, unless they knew a secret passage leading out of the cave, to have perished there."

Again Pant thought of the ancient treasure they must have carried with them.

"Did the savage tribe follow them into the cave?"

"They were afraid. That's the way the

story goes. Afraid the Earth God of the Mayas would push the mountain down upon them if they should enter."

" So," thought Pant, " whatever the Mayas took with them is in the cave still. And they were possessed of great wealth. I have read of it. Gold and jade, topaz and perhaps diamonds, pearls from the western shores and strange little gods carved from rare stones or formed from metal."

All this he thought, but not one word did he say as they resumed their upward march.

The entrance to the cave, which they reached after much climbing, was most picturesque. Its mouth was entirely hidden by dark spreading palm leaves. A sparkling stream, appearing to emerge from nowhere, went dashing headlong over a rocky ledge.

Parting the large leaves as if they had been a curtain, the boys peered within to find there a dark hole from which there came a constant draft of cool damp air.

" Boo!" said Pant. "It's cold in there."

The other boy did not hear him. He was staring in amazement at his black servant. As if seized by a sudden fit of ague, the giant was shaking violently from head to foot.

"A chill," said Pant as he caught sight of him.

"Afraid," his companion whispered back. "Afraid of the Earth God of the Mayas. He has great courage and the strength of three. I have never known him to fear anything before."

In a moment it became evident that the black man was ashamed of his fear and was making brave attempts to conquer it. In the end he won and, seating himself upon a rock, watched his young master and Pant remove their shoes and stockings. The narrow entrance to the cave offered no footing save the moss covered rocks at the bottom of the stream.

As they signified their readiness to start, the black lifted the door of a strange glassless lantern of beaten brass which, Pant was told, burned fish oil and would provide a feeble light for hours on end. After lighting the lantern he plunged boldly into the stream and led the way through icy water straight into the darkness of night until, with a grunt of satisfaction, he emerged panting and dripping upon a dry ledge where the cave suddenly widened to a broad chamber.

For a time, lighted only by the dull gleam of the Carib's lantern, they moved along the brink of the narrow stream. The silence was oppressive. The stream flowed placidly over an all but level floor, making no sound. Only the gentle pat-pat of their bare feet disturbed the tomb-like hush that hung over all.

Then of a sudden, like thunder from a clear sky, pandemonium broke loose. The innocent cause of all the commotion was the Carib. He had, by chance, struck his lantern against a rock.

The air was filled with strange noises, such a whirring and snapping as not one of them had heard before.

"Wha—what is it?" Kirk's hand trembled as he gripped Pant's arm.

"Bats," said Pant. "Stand perfectly still. They will settle."

For a single second he threw on his flashlight and allowed it to play across the space before them. The other boy's eyes went big with wonder. Even Pant, who had seen much of Central American life, was astonished. Bats, a million of them it seemed, circled the air. And such bats! No tiny mouse-like creatures were these, but great gray monsters with broad spreading wings, gleaming eyes and teeth that shone white in the perpetual night about them.

"Don't." Kirk's hand was on his arm. The light flashed out.

"May as well go ahead," said Pant. "Doubt if they go far back into the cave."

They had not gone a hundred yards before they came to a very narrow passage. Once more they were obliged to take to the bed of the stream. This lasted only a moment. As they emerged there came over them a sense of vastness. Was it the quality of silence that was there? Was it the changed sound of their footsteps? Or was it some sixth sense that told them? As Pant threw the gleam of his powerful flashlight before them, an exclamation escaped every lip.

Nothing they had seen in any land could compare with the splendor of the masonry of the vast cathedral that lay before them.

Masonry? This indeed they at first thought it, the work of some great lost race. In time they came to realize that the splendid gleaming pillars were the work of time and a great Creator, the Master Builders of all ages. The pillars were great stalagmites, formed by the dripping of water through a thousand thousand years.

Strangest of all, as they listened they caught from afar a sound that was like music.

"Like some mighty organ played softly while a thousand children chant," Kirk whispered.

It was now time to cover their feet, yet even the Carib felt something of the awe that led the others on, still barefooted.

The illusion of the chant could not last forever. As they advanced the sound increased in volume, became more distinct until it burst upon them as the rush and roar of a miniature cataract, where the stream emerged from a chamber still beyond.

" Shall we go on? " Pant stood with his feet in the lower water of the cataract.

" If—if we don't get lost," the younger boy hesitated.

" Not a chance," said Pant. " We have only to follow the stream back."

" To be sure. How stupid of me. Yes, let's go on." There was an eager note in Kirk's voice. Pant read it correctly. He was eager to go forward for, in some hidden chamber, perhaps just beyond, there might rest a vast treasure from the forgotten past.

The ascent of the water worn and slippery rocks was difficult. More than once the younger boy was in danger of being thrown into the torrent of water, but drawn on by Pant, lifted forward now and then by the giant black, he made his way upward until with a sigh of relief he dropped upon dry sand at the head of the waterfall. Once more Pant's light gleamed out before them. Fresh marvels awaited them. A vast, silent underground lake, reaching as far as the light would carry and yet beyond, seemed to beckon them on.

Switching off his light, that batteries might be saved for a possible emergency, Pant followed the Carib and his dim light along the shore of this new marvel.

They had gone two hundred yards or more when out of the darkness before them, on the shore of the lake, something loomed indistinct and gray.

" What is it? " The younger boy came to a sudden halt.

" We'll see." There came the snap of Pant's flashlight.

The next instant, as if pushed by a sudden force, they all fell back. Before them, drawn up on the beach, with paddles crossed over the seat, was a light canoe.

Staring with all their eyes, they stood there expecting any moment to see the mysterious canoeist emerge from the dim distance beyond.

Not knowing what to think, Pant stood at attention. As he did so, a strange chattering struck his ears. Wheeling about, he discovered the cause. The black giant's teeth were chattering. Once more he was shaking from head to foot. His face was almost white with fear.

CHAPTER III

A STRANGE DARK ROOM

Not knowing what else to do as he stood before the canoe, Pant laughed. The laugh did not ring quite true, but it served the purpose for which it was intended. It broke the spell.

" Come on," he said. " Let's see."

A few strides and he stood beside the mysterious craft.

" Dust," he said, dragging his fingers across the seat. " Probably been here for a hundred, two hundred years."

" How wonderfully preserved it is," said Kirk.

" Those people knew the secret of preserving wood by boiling it in certain kinds of oil. They knew a great deal more that might well have been kept by the white man. But the

47

type of Spaniard who came to these shores, as well as the wild barbarians who came before them, were all for gold."

As he stood there beside this strange underground sea, with this relic of another age so close beside him, Pant found himself lost in revery. He was trying to reproduce through his mind's eye the scenes that these silent waters might once have witnessed.

"What a unique picnic ground," he said to Kirk. "One sees it still. Gleaming torches, moving like giant firebugs across the water; dark canoes gliding here and there; the joyous shouts of children that came echoing back."

"Hello-o!" he shouted suddenly. Back across the water it came to him again and again. "Hello-o—H-e-l-l-o-o-o."

"Perhaps there are fish," he went on. "May be very large fish. Blind, because there is no need of eyes, but fine fish all the same. Can you see them, the little Indian boys fishing from their canoes? Can you catch the gleam of their campfires as they roasted their fish over the coals?"

He kicked the beach under his feet and sure enough, from beneath the dust of centuries he uncovered the ashes of a long burned out fire.

"You see," he smiled, "I am a conjurer. I can read both the past and the future."

"Then," said the other boy with a little shudder and a doubtful smile, "tell us what happens next."

"Next?" said Pant. "Why next we find a small room equipped with a table and some chairs. I have some work to do in such a place, in fact that's what I came for. I needed a dark room. But this," he spread his arm wide, "this is not a room; it is a whole hidden world."

Turning without another word, the other boy beckoned to the great Carib, who had regained his composure, and together they skirted the shore of the lake to penetrate deeper into the hidden mysteries of the mountain.

Again the chamber narrowed. Again they were obliged to take to the bed of the stream.

This time, to Pant's great joy, they emerged into a small room walled and pillared in spotless white.

"The very place!" he exclaimed. "To be sure, there are no real chairs or table, but that heap of fallen stalactites will take their place, and there is water in abundance. Have a seat. I will be through before you know it."

Unwrapping his pack, he drew forth the fibre trays. These he filled with water. Having placed them upon a circular fragment of stalactite that offered a level surface like the top of a round table, he shook a powder into one, a second powder into another, and left the other crystal clear and pure.

After stirring the powder for a time, he drew forth a red cloth and wound it twice round the Carib's lantern.

The effect was startling. At once the glistening white stalactites and stalagmites were turned blood red. The Carib struggled hard against the wild fears and superstitions within him, conquered in the end, to sit impassive, watching.

Opening his black box, Pant removed a square of film. Having dropped this into the first tray, he began rocking it slowly back and forth.

"A picture!" exclaimed Kirk. "Do you mean to tell me you have come all this way to develop a picture?"

"There was no other dark room. And besides," said Pant, "this picture is important, the most important bit of work I have done in a long time. Upon its success hangs my good old grandfather's entire fortune.

"You see," he went on, as he continued to rock the tray, "through influential friends my grandfather secured a valuable concession, the right to gather chicle on a large tract of government land. This tract is bordered on one side by the holdings of the Central Chicle Company, a powerful and jealous corporation. This company is honest, but perhaps they are unscrupulous in their competition. Who can tell? Perhaps they would drive my grandfather to the wall if they could."

Had not the red light hid it, he might have seen a crimson flush suffuse the other boy's face as he spoke these words. It was lost upon him.

"Our tract," he went on, "is bordered on the other side by land owned by an unscrupulous Spaniard.

"We received a map from England showing the boundaries of our holdings. It had not been in the office a week when it was stolen. Without it our hands were tied. If we attempted to work our concession without knowing the true unfenced boundaries we were sure to infringe upon the rights of our neighbors. If we did not they would claim we had, and would ruin us with claims for indemnities.

"If we did not have the map back within a very short time—" he paused to hold the square of film to the light. A little cry of joy escaped his lips. " It's coming! I've got them! See those dark spots, three of them?"

The other boy nodded.

" Three men," he said impressively.

He dropped the film into the developing bath to resume his story. " I told grandfather to wait, I would get the map. I went straight back into the bush where the crafty Spaniard has his camp. It was dangerous, but I know the bush. I was careful. I took my camera and a flashlight outfit with me. Fortune was with me. I came upon the Spaniard and two of his men examining the map at night. They were inside a bamboo cabin. I put my camera to a crack, opened the shutter, touched off a flash, and at once was away. That is how I came to the home of your Spanish friends. That is why I am here. And there," he said, holding the film by its corners, " is the picture. And it is far better than I hoped for."

The film was indeed a strong and clear one. The crafty faces of the Spaniards and the square map stood out in bold relief.

" Just a touch more," he sighed as he dipped it carefully in the solution.

" You see," he added in conclusion, " all we need to do is to get an enlargement made. That will give us a perfect map showing all the boundaries. What's more, it gives us proof that they stole the map."

" I am glad," said Kirk, " that it was not the big American Company who stole it."

" Oh, they wouldn't do that," said Pant quickly. " But why are you glad?"

The other boy did not reply. A moment of silence followed. Pant dropped his film into the washing tray, then began rocking it again.

Moments passed. Only the drip-drip of water in some distant corner of the cave and the all but inaudible rush of the stream disturbed the silence of the place.

" There!" Pant breathed at last as he dropped the film into the fixing bath. " We can have more light now. How would you like to take your man here and go into the chamber just beyond while I finish this job? No harm can come of it, and you might discover something of real interest."

For a moment the younger boy hesitated. Then, as if struck by a sudden thought, he said, " Yes. Why not? "

A moment later Pant saw the shadows of his two companions in adventure moving jerkily along the gleaming walls.

" Like ghosts," he thought. Something like a tremor ran down his spine.

He turned to attend to his film. When he looked again they were gone. Instantly he regretted his suggestion.

" Spooky business, being here alone in this cave," he thought. " Dark and damp—sort of like a tomb. Who knows how many human beings have perished here? This cave is their tombstone and their vault. How still it is! " Listening, he thought he heard his own heart beat. " What would I do if they failed to return? Go in search of them, I suppose. And then? "

He did not like to think of exploring the place alone. All well enough with others, but alone? Well, anyway, one likes company in such a place.

The fixing bath was done with. For the final washing he chose a still pool at the side of the stream. As he dropped in the film, a tiny fish, startled from its place of hiding, suddenly leaped clear of the water. The effect on the boy was startling. He jumped backward, and nearly fell into the stream.

"Bah!" he exclaimed, quite put out at himself. "How absurd! Nerves. Have to find something to do."

Having completed the washing of the film, he fitted it into a protecting frame, then closed two trays over it and bound the whole tight. He finished by repacking the kit.

This done, he allowed his eyes to wander here and there about the place. "Have a look," he told himself. Instantly some object in a distant corner, quite well up on a broken ledge, caught his attention.

"Strange!" he murmured. "Doesn't look quite natural. Unusual color. Have a look." He started toward the corner, then paused. A curious tremor shot through him. It was as if he had been on board a ship that had rolled ever so lightly in a trough of the sea.

"Nonsense!" he muttered. "Nerves." He again moved toward the corner.

At that very moment, as often happens when one stands facing some strange and mysterious phenomenon, Pant thought of one who was far away, his good pal Johnny Thompson.

He thought, too, of the strange message of figures and signs he had left in the office at Stann Creek. He wondered if Johnny had found it yet. If so, had he read it? Premonitions of some happening tremendous and terrifying were passing through his mind. If disaster overtook him here, would Johnny decipher the note? Would he come in search of him? Would he ultimately find him? So his thoughts whirled on.

CHAPTER IV

JOHNNY THOMPSON IN JAIL

It may seem a trifle strange that anything could have separated these good pals, Johnny and Pant. Fact is, only Pant's discovery of a genuine blood relative, his grandfather, could have brought about such separation. Pant of course had become deeply engrossed in the work of building up the fortune of his white-haired grandsire. In this task Johnny had shown a lively interest until the concession with the priceless map enclosed had arrived. From that time on, it had seemed, nothing remained to be done save to round up a band of chicleros and get back into the bush. There a camp would be built and long weeks spent in gathering and boiling down the sap of the "chewing gum" trees. For this task Johnny had no taste. He must have adventure.

So on that bright tropical morning, little dreaming that the safe would be robbed that night and that adventure would be provided for all, he had cut himself a stout stick for dealing with snakes, had strapped a machete to his belt and had fared forth alone in search of adventure.

Had Johnny lived in Honduras twenty-five years, or even ten, he would have waited for the train. It wouldn't go up for two days. But always, to the Central American, there is plenty of time.

But Johnny was new to the Tropics. He was in the habit of taking the best transportation he could get. The best this time was a pair of short sturdy legs which belonged to Johnny Thompson.

The road leads through a jungle. Here and there is a small group of struggling, insignificant banana plantations, but the jungle has so far succeeded in taking them back to itself that they, too, seem wild.

There is a certain joy to be had from a journey on foot through a tropical jungle. There is a glimmer of green, a fresh damp odor of decay, faint and pleasing as musk, and there always comes from the bushes and trees a suggestion of low, joyous music, made, perhaps by bees and birds, but nevertheless it is there, an indescribable music. Johnny had enjoyed all this until he had begun to feel the need of food and refreshment. Most of all, he wanted a drink. Any old drink would do. But there was no drink. The dry season was nearing its close. Everywhere the floor of the jungle was dry as the Sahara.

Had Johnny lived long in the jungle he would have stepped aside to break the stem of a certain plant, then to catch in the hollow of his hand the delicious water that came dripping out almost in a stream.

He hadn't lived long in a jungle, so all he could do was to plod on.

When his desire for water had become intense longing, when his tongue seemed to fill his mouth and his throat clicked when he swallowed, he had found himself by a sudden turn to the right brought suddenly into the midst of an orchard of fruit trees.

"Forbidden fruit" is the name the natives have given these great golden balls. Johnny didn't call them that. He had called them grapefruit. He hadn't eaten grapefruit many times because he had found them bitter.

"Bitter!" he had said, making a wry face. "Bitter, and me dying of thirst!" At a distance they had looked like oranges.

"Oh well—" He had resigned himself to his fate. "Here goes!"

He had left the railway bed, then dropping on the moss beneath a heavily laden tree, had seized upon a great golden ball and had begun tearing away its covering.

Having quartered the fruit, he had made up a wry face and thrust a generous wedge into his mouth.

Instantly the wry face had vanished. A glorious smile took its place.

"Not bad," he said, filling his mouth again.

"Not half bad. Just need to get ripe, I suppose. Sugar would be an insult to such fruit as this. People in the States don't know what it is."

He had spoken to himself, but some one else had heard, for from somewhere above him there had come in a melodious voice:

"So you like forbidden fruit?"

"I—I beg your pardon!" Johnny was on his feet at once. "I—I didn't mean to steal. See here, I'll buy a quarter's worth."

He had looked up at the girl whose golden hair, golden freckles and dark green dress so completely blended with fruit and foliage that, until now, he had not seen her.

"Have you a donkey?" There was a suggestion of a laugh in the girl's tone. "I don't see any."

"Why must I have a donkey?" Johnny looked his surprise.

"Because we sell them by the barrel. Fifty cents a barrel. Of course, for a quarter you'd only get a half a barrel. But even so, how

are you going to carry them?" Shaking out
her dress and laughing the girl had dropped
to the ground.

Out of his little adventure in the grapefruit
orchard had grown a new enterprise. Johnny
suddenly decided to become a shipping agent.
Madge Kennedy, who had turned out to be a
Scotch girl, had insisted upon his accompany-
ing her to the house to meet her grandfather,
Donald Kennedy. The grandfather, a great
gray-bearded man with a store of knowledge
that could come only from long study and
many years in the jungle, had proven a find
indeed. Johnny did not soon tire of sitting
on the broad veranda of the long one-story
house, listening to the old man as he rambled
on about bananas and grapefruit, strange
tropical foods, Carib Indians, and the future
of their little Central American Colony.

It had not taken Johnny long to discover,
however, that these kindly people were really
almost paupers in the midst of their abundance. Many carloads of the finest fruit in the

world hung ripe on the trees. Why was it not being shipped?

When he had pressed them for an answer to this puzzling question, Madge Kennedy had told him that the fruit company had refused to accept their fruit. The reason, she supposed, was that her grandfather had two years before sold his crop to the owner of a tramp steamer. The great East Sea Fruit Company, which had a monopoly on the fruit trade of Central America, did not wish competition, and they took this method of punishing her grandfather.

"But say!" Johnny leaped to his feet. "I'll find you a ship. There's one anchored off Belize now. Jorgensen is the captain. He's anxious enough for a cargo. Came all this way for a cargo of mahogany. The half-caste Indian woodcutters are on a strike. There is no mahogany to haul."

"Oh!" Madge beamed upon him in sudden excitement.

"But then," her smile vanished, "I know

the ship. It's no use. We have only a third of a cargo for her."

" Finish up with bananas," Johnny suggested.

" Whose bananas? Every grower has a contract to sell only to the Fruit Company."

For a little time Johnny felt himself baffled, defeated. Then of a sudden an inspiration came. Many times he had watched the loading of bananas off the dock at Stann Creek.

" Six hands!" he exclaimed excitedly. "That's it! Six hands! We'll have a cargo yet!"

That very night, after telling Madge of his grand plan, he started for Guatemala City to see the man who owned the largest banana plantation in Central America.

For some little time fortune smiled upon him in his new enterprise. Arriving at Stann Creek in the dead of night he found a sailing boat preparing to leave for Porte Barrios. At this port he caught a train for Guatemala.

High noon found him walking the streets of that ancient and most beautiful city of Central America.

The city's beauty was lost **upon** him. His thoughts were centered about one man, Don del Valle, the richest banana grower in all that land. He at once went about the task of finding the man and securing an interview. Having discovered the dapper, black-eyed Guatemalan sitting in his garden sipping wine, he wasted no time on ceremony but, boy-like, launched at once into his project.

The astonished del Valle, who understood only a part of what was said and who was accustomed to inflict long periods of waiting and numerous delays, stared at him in astonishment for a time. Then he demanded:

"What is it that this mad boy wants?"

"Bananas! I want bananas!" Johnny exclaimed.

"Well then, go and buy them, as many as you like." del Valle threw a handful of coppers at his feet.

"But I want many. Two-thirds of a ship load, twenty thousand bunches." Johnny's face took on an air of unusual seriousness.

"But I have no bananas to sell. They are contracted for, as you should know, by your great American company."

"But not the six hands." Johnny exclaimed eagerly. "I only ask for six hands."

"Six hands!" the Guatemalan exclaimed in a fit of passion. "Six hands! Here, take this crazy youth to jail. I will prefer a charge of annoying a gentleman."

The two native policemen, who were in reality the official guard of the great gentleman, sprang into action. Ten minutes later Johnny found himself inside looking out, and the window he looked through was heavily barred. So it was that Johnny Thompson came to be in jail.

CHAPTER V

TOTTERING WALLS

It was at an early hour of that same night that Johnny, having wakened from some vaguely remembered dream, found himself rudely \shaken by a strange convulsion beneath and about him.

"Ship's pitching something terrible," he told himself. "Must be a hurricane."

"Ship?" something within him seemed to whisper. "Ship? When did you embark upon a ship?"

Vaguely he groped about in his brain for facts. The sensations that come to one just before he falls asleep are, more often than not, awaiting him when he awakes. Johnny's had remained with him. They were earth sensations, solid earth, a place close and stuffy, and stone, solid stone, not shifting sea.

But there was now a strange rocking and shuddering, no mistake about that. There it was again! Zowie! What a lurch!

" Like a ship at sea in a storm," he told himself. " No, not quite. More like a ship stuck fast on a coral reef, being beaten to pieces by the waves."

The thought was startling. Again he attempted to sit up. This time he succeeded.

Light streamed down upon him, moonlight broken into little squares.

" Bars," he thought. " Prison bars! "

Yes, now he remembered. This bed, not a bed at all, merely a broad ledge of stone left by the prison masons in lieu of a bed. Strange sort, these Central American prisons!

Then, as if to refute all this, there came again that horrible rocking shudder.

Struggling to grasp reality, Johnny's eyes, roving the dark spaces about him, arrived at the crisscross iron bars of the window. To his vast astonishment he saw those iron bars, in a solid mass, literally torn from the masonry.

"I don't know where I am," he told himself, "but I won't be there very long."

With one thought uppermost in his mind, that of escape, he leaped for the window, gripped the sill, drew himself up, balanced for a second there in the moonlight, then dropped.

He landed rather solidly, not upon the tossing sea, but upon tossing dry land.

A moving figure loomed before him.

"A guard!" His quickened senses registered the thought.

"Strike first, and talk afterwards." His head buried itself into the soft center of the moving object. With a grunt the man went down.

He wished the earth would stand still. It made him seasick, that rocking motion. They hadn't had a reason for putting him in prison —not any real reason. He had done nothing except insist upon buying twenty thousand bunches of bananas. He had tried to do a great service to a splendid old man and a beautiful girl. He had reason enough for wanting to be out of prison, plenty of reasons. There was the girl, Madge Kennedy, back there in the orchard of forbidden fruit, and her grandfather, the aged Britisher who was so much of a man and so little of a business man that his orchards and banana plantations would never make him a cent unless some one took a hand. And there was old Jorgensen, good old salt water skipper, walking his deck night and day and staring gloomily at the Caribbean Sea.

The earth stopped rocking for an instant. An open court lay before him. He was beginning to realize that he was having a new experience. One of those frequent Central American earthquakes had broken loose. That was why a stone prison had seemed so like a ship on a tossing sea.

" Open places are best," he told himself.

He had taken ,a dozen steps when there came a shock which sent him down like a tenpin. At the same instant he touched an object lying near him.

He found it soft and yielding. It was a weeping child, a beautiful, black-haired, black-eyed girl of seven.

" There now," he said, sitting up and talking quietly to her. " The storm will pass in a short while. We're not shipping any water. She's a staunch old barge. We'll weather this little blow and never lose a mast or a yardarm."

Since the girl was unquestionably Spanish, it seems probable that she understood not one word that he said. She did understand the steady comforting tone and the kindly touch of his hand. She stopped crying, cuddled down in his arms and, since it was now well into night, she fell asleep.

As Johnny sat there, a motley throng gathered about him. Like him, they came to this open spot for safety. Some, like himself, were fully dressed. Some were in pajamas. The mild moonlight was kind to these last. Some carried things in their hands, things they had salvaged from the doom of their homes. A parrot in a cage, an iron strong box, an alarm clock, a broom; these and many more things, somber, precious, ludicrous, had been brought into the open plaza.

Johnny's mind began to travel back, to gather up the slender thread of circumstances that had brought him there. He traced it thread by thread. " To-morrow," he told himself, " will bring something quite new."

CHAPTER VI

AN EARTHQUAKE WITHIN A CAVE

After leaving Pant to complete his photographic work, Kirk and his giant servant had passed from the small chamber to one very much larger. He had taken one of Pant's flashlights. As he sent its gleam down the chamber he found it impossible 'to see the distant wall. The ceiling was low, so low that he was obliged to stoop at times to clear it. The stalactites and stalagmites were found in such numbers that they formed a veritable labyrinth.

"Mustn't go far," he told himself. "Might be difficult to find our way back."

At that moment, as his flashlight painted a white avenue between two rows of natural pillars, he caught a strange yellow gleam a short way before him on the floor.

A few steps and he was at the spot. His hand was on the thing, an ornament of gold of elaborate design, when his foot struck something that crushed in like an ancient gourd.

One horrified glance, and he sprang back. "A skull. A human skull!" he breathed.

One instant of horror, then he knew where they were, or at least thought he knew. They had found the final resting place of a race that had vanished from the earth.

A moment's poking about in the dust convinced him that this was true. Human bones mingled with gold and silver ornaments, pots of bronze, strings of jade beads, and who knows what other priceless treasures from the past, formed a setting for a bit of drama at once shocking and intriguing.

Scarcely knowing what he was about, like some child in Fairyland, he began gathering up handfuls of the most attractive trinkets and thrusting them into the deep pockets of his knickers.

It was while he was engaged in this strange occupation that he felt the same curious sensation that had come to Pant.

" It—why, it's like—" His heart raced wildly. " It's as if the world had tipped a little ! "

Instantly he heard the loud chatter of the giant's teeth. In the midst of the chatter he caught the sound of an attempted chant, the Carib chant which they, in their darkness of mind, believe will drive away evil spirits.

The boy gathered no other trinkets. A moment passed, another and another. Every tick of his wrist watch sounded out in the dead silence of the place like the tolling of a funeral bell.

Then, of a sudden, pandemonium broke loose. The earth rocked. Huge stalactites came crashing down, to roll about the floor like barrels on the deck of a tossing ship. A grinning skull rolled at his feet. With his head in a whirl, Kirk knew not whether to stand or to flee.

" The earth god of the Mayas! " a terrible voice sounded in his ear. It was the Carib's voice. The next moment a powerful arm encircled him and he was whirled through the dark.

His senses reeled. Only dimly could he realize what was passing. There was an earthquake. He was sure of that. They were common enough in Central America. They had been caught in a cave while an earthquake was in progress. What could be more terrible? The big black man, ever faithful to his trust, was attempting to carry him out.

*   *   *   *   *

Pant, who had mistaken the first strange tilting of that portion of the earth's surface on which he stood as no movement at all but a break of the imagination based on unstrung nerves, had moved with a rare showing of determination toward the curious object which lay on the rocky shelf. He had made it out as a small chest some two feet long and a foot deep. He had discovered that the top was thickly encrusted with dust, but the sides had the appearance of some beaten metal, stained and corroded by age. This much he had learned when the sudden shock of the earthquake came.

If the first movement had seemed like the sudden lifting of a ship by a heavy sea, the second was like the shudder and crash of a great ocean liner as she is thrown upon the rocks in a mighty storm.

The first shock left him well nigh senseless. The second brought reason back upon its throne. He thought at once of his young companion. He had brought him to this place and somehow he must see that he escaped from this awful thing that was going on.

Seizing his flashlight, he started forward. At once he thought of his water-proof package and of the precious negative it contained.

" I owe much to my grandfather. Can't lose that," he thought.

Groping his way back, he secured the package. Then, turning his face resolutely toward the spot where the other boy and his black servant had vanished, he pushed forward. He had gone a dozen paces, had barely escaped being crushed by a ponderous pillar of white crystal, when a sudden quake brought him to his knees.

Instantly he was up and fighting his way forward. And now his eyes fell upon the opening through which his companions had gone.

What was his horror when at that moment there came a crashing and grinding sound, dust filled the air until he could scarcely see; yet through it all one fact stood out clear and undisputable. The opening through which the others had gone was closed.

Next moment some object hurtling at him from the right, striking him squarely, sent him crashing to earth. There, bruised, half senseless, he all but gave himself over to despair.

Through the moment of hopelessness which overcame the boy shot one ray of light. This light, shining brighter and brighter, brought him courage to battle on. That light was the sudden realization that God, the one true God, the good, patient, just God, was still in his universe and that He still noted the sparrow's fall.

The instant this fact was established, the boy's mind grew calm. One calm thought led to another. What had struck him? Not a rock. That would have crushed him. What, then? What but a human being.

"The giant black!" he thought.

At that moment he caught a wavering gleam of light. It was in the direction of the cave's entrance.

"The black," he said again. "They escaped. Thank—thank God!"

Instantly he was away, following the light.

For a moment the rude shocks of the earthquake were over. Aside from the debris that had been scattered about, his progress was unimpeded, yet he made no gain on the feeble light that wavered on before him.

"Didn't suppose that boy could travel so fast," he told himself.

Instantly a thought set him shuddering. Had the black servant, overcome by a terrible fear of a heathen god, forsaken his young charge? How was he to know? For a second he hesitated, then redoubled his pace.

"Overtake him and force him to go back," he told himself. "If—"

He hoped his fears were unfounded.

He came to the entrance of the great underground lake chamber, had passed it in safety and was skirting the shore of the lake, which was recovering from a great agitation, when the earth shudder began again.

Battling against the dizziness that seemed about to overcome him, stumbling, all but falling, he had fought his way forward until at last the great bulk of the black man stood out before him. Then, as the very universe appeared to reel, a great tidal wave from the lake came sweeping over him.

Strangely enough, at that moment there

came into his mind a picture of his grandfather's face. He thought of the water-proof package and the precious negative, and gripped them tight.

The tidal wave receded. It did not return. He found himself once more on solid ground and close by, not twenty yards away, was the black and his young master. This last onslaught had been too much for the giant native. His knees had given way beneath him and he had slumped to earth, murmuring incoherent things about the earth god of the Mayas.

As for Pant and Kirk, they knew no fear of Maya gods. They waited, and as they stood there they felt the rude shocks no more. The surface of the lake was again as placid as a pond beneath a silvery moon.

They made their way forward in silence until, with a little thrill of joy, the younger boy gripped his companion's arm as he cried:

"See! The light! The light of the moon!" It was true. They had reached the entrance.

A moment more and they were sitting in the shadows beneath the palms.

"See!" said Kirk at last, drawing from his pocket an object that gleamed in the sunlight. "A message from out the past."

It was indeed an interesting collection he had gathered quite at random. A bracelet of gold set with jade, a small bronze god, grinning and terrible, a miniature silver goblet, and some other bits of jewelry of such odd design that one was not able to so much as guess their purpose.

"Sometime," said Kirk, "we will go back for more."

"I doubt if you will ever enter that chamber again," said Pant. "I believe the earthquake closed the entrance to that particular chamber. But we will go back.

"Oh yes, we will go back," he repeated a moment later. He was thinking of the strange chest that was all but within his grasp when the earth shudder came.

"But now," said Kirk, "we must go down.

Morning will soon be here. And think what the earthquake must have done to the old Don's castle! Come!" he cried, shuddering with a terrible apprehension. "Our good friends may be buried beneath the ruins of their home—they may be dead!"

Closely followed by Pant and the great Carib, he sprang away down the ancient trail.

CHAPTER VII

JOHNNY WINS A FRIEND

Just as the first faint glow of dawn lighted the shattered walls and yawning windows of the ancient Guatemalan jail from which Johnny Thompson had been so strangely released, the Spanish child in his arms stirred, then sat up to stare about her. At that moment a tall, dark Honduran came walking rapidly across the plaza.

"Don del Valle!" Johnny started. This was the man who owned a fifth of all the banana land in Central America, the man who had ordered him thrown into jail.

"What next?" he thought.

Not knowing whether to break and run, or stand his ground, he hesitated until the man was upon him.

"Hah!" the man exclaimed. "At last!"

Johnny was on his feet in an instant, prepared for flight. "He's been looking for me," his thoughts raced on. "Now he's found me, he'll find me another jail. He'll put me in. If he can catch me. He can't." Yet for the moment he stood still. Why? Probably he did not know why, but it was well that he did not run.

"Where did you find the child?" This was the question the dark-skinned de Valle shot at Johnny. At the same instant the child Johnny had protected during the terrifying earthquake sprang into the Honduran's arms. The man's tone was not harsh as it had been the night before.

"Why I—" Johnny tried to think. "I really didn't find her. She found—that is, we fell over each other, so we decided to camp here until the earth began standing still."

"But you, my young friend? You are in jail. Is it not so?"

"I was in jail." Johnny felt a creepy sensation running up his back. That had been a terribly uncomfortable jail. "The—the jail wasn't safe,"—his face twisted into a quizzical smile—" so I came over here to the plaza."

As he spoke the child was pouring words, soft melodious Spanish words into Don del Valle's ears.

" I am sorry," said the Honduran. " I was hasty. You should not have gone to jail. My child here, who was lost from us in the catastrophe, tells me you were her protector. You have returned me good for evil. Pardon. You wished to ask me something? Bananas, was it not? You should know that I have no bananas to sell, that they are all contracted for by your American fruit company."

Johnny's heart leaped. Luck was coming his way. Providence had sent him an earthquake to cast down his prison bars and a child to plead his cause. Before his mind's eye came the faces of good old Kennedy, of Madge Kennedy and of Captain Jorgensen. He might be able to help them yet. At any rate he was not to go back to jail.

"But you don't understand," he found himself saying to the rich Spaniard. "It is only
the six hands I ask. They are not contracted
for. Two-thirds of a ship load is all I need."

"Ah! Six hands you say." Don del Valle
stroked his beard. "It might be arranged."

"But you are hungry!" he exclaimed.
"The walls of my house are cracked, but it
has not fallen. The great shudder is over,
please God. My servants have cleared away
the rubbish and put things to right. We will
have coffee and hot corn cakes in the garden.
After that we will talk of these six hands.
Come!"

He led the way through streets strewn with
debris. The child, flitting back and forth like
a sunbeam, placed a confiding hand first in
Johnny's, then in her father's brown palm.

In spite of the havoc wrought by the earthquake, Don del Valle's garden was still very
beautiful. The broken fragments of a great
flower-filled urn had been cleared away. Two
fallen trees still lay prone amid a blazing bed

of flowering plants. In the background, in the midst of a luxuriant growth of strange tropical and semi-tropical plants, a path led to inviting realms beyond.

On a broad piazza they sat in rosewood chairs around tables of solid mahogany, munching hot corn cakes and sipping coffee. There was Don del Valle and his wife, a very beautiful Spanish lady. Besides Johnny and the little girl, there were no others.

" She is their only child," thought Johnny as he noted how tenderly they cared for the dark-eyed girl. " What a privilege to show her a kindness."

The talk ran on about matters quite foreign to business. They speculated regarding the extent of damage done by the earthquake and the area shaken by it.

" And have you many earthquakes in the United States? " asked the lady.

" I have never experienced one before," Johnny replied. " Our land is very broad and flat. It has little backbone. Mountains are the backbone of the land. At times the backbone appears to shake up a bit."

"Ah yes!" said the Don. "It is quite true. Our land is very much backbone, almost nothing else."

Johnny was interested in everything that these people had to say, but was very anxious to get down to business. He had come to purchase bananas, twenty thousand bunches at least. There was need of haste. Skipper Jorgensen's ship, the *North Star,* was lying before Belize in British Honduras without a cargo—at least it had been lying there three days before. There was no telling at what moment some one might offer him a cargo of cocoanuts, chicle, mahogany or a combination cargo of all. Then Johnny's chance of helping Kennedy and his granddaughter by getting off their year's crop of grapefruit would be gone.

"And that," he told himself, "would be a great tragedy."

"And now," said his host, as the others

moved away and the servant disappeared with the dishes, " we may talk. We must make it brief. I am a busy man. In this city I operate two stores, a cotton mill and a warehouse. I must find out at once the extent of damage done by the shock. You want bananas?"

" Six hand bunches."

" Ah yes, you wish only the six hand bunches. And how can you use six hand bunches? The Fruit Company will never purchase them. How can you hope to dispose of them? They are not used. Either they are not gathered at all, or they are given to the stevedores or are cut up and cast into the sea."

" That's just it," said Johnny, leaning eagerly forward. " It was just because you do not care for them, because you have no contract with the Fruit Company to deliver them, that I thought you would be willing to sell them to me."

" Sell them!" The man's eyes lighted. " I could almost give them to you. Five cents a bunch. That would pay for gathering and bringing them to the wharf. But you?" He turned his eyes upon the boy. "What will you do with them? If the Fruit Company cannot handle them, how can you?

"You see," he smiled, "because you were kind to my child, I like you. I do not wish to see you cheat yourself."

"Look!" said Johnny, rising to pace the stone floor. "You grade your bananas according to the number of groups on a stem. You call those groups hands. For a bunch having seven hands the Fruit Company pays twenty-five cents; eight hands thirty-seven and a half; nine hands or more fifty cents. If a bunch has only six hands they will not buy it. Is it not so?"

"*Si, Si, Senor.* It is true."

"But are the bananas on the six hand bunch smaller? Are they less sweet? Will they spoil more quickly than those on the other bunches?"

"No, *Senor.*"

"Then why are they not as good?"

The Spaniard shrugged his shoulders for reply.

"They are as good, exactly as good!" Johnny struck the table with his open palm. "Small bunches are a little more trouble to handle. That is the only difference. There are plenty larger. The Fruit Company takes only what it wishes and reaps a rich reward from this. But we will handle the six hand bunches.

"In America," his tone became quiet, "there are thousands of poor people who would gladly eat more bananas. Their children love them. Do they eat them? No. Why? Because, while you sell a bunch, one hundred bananas, for a quarter, in the United States one must pay a quarter for five.

"There may be legitimate reasons for the great difference in price. I am not going to look into that. It is not my task. But for once, in a little corner of our great country, there will be cheap bananas. Six hand bunches. You sell them to me for five cents a bunch and I will do the rest. How many may I have? Twenty thousand bunches?"

"Twenty-five thousand, *Senor.* On my three plantations there are this many small bunches. You may have them all. I will give you a note to my manager at Porte Zalaya. He will have them brought to the docks at once."

"In regard to the pay, I—"

"You will pay when your people pay you for the bananas," said the generous Spaniard. "Send me a draft. If the money does not come to you, then it will never come to me.

"And now," he said, "I must go. Come inside, and I will instruct my secretary about the note you are to carry to my manager at Porte Zalaya."

Ten minutes later, stepping on air, Johnny made his way toward the railway station.

"Now," he said to himself, "if only I can reach the *North Star* before Captain Jorgensen contracts for another cargo, all is well. I'll make it snappy."

He had not lived in Central America long enough to know that in this little world of sudden revolution and many strange surprises, things are almost never done snappy. It is the land of *manana* (tomorrow), a land where nearly everyone believes that *manana* will do very well for all " snappy " business.

CHAPTER VIII

AN ANCIENT CASTLE IN RUINS

The moon was still casting a golden glow over the wonders of a tropical world when Pant and Kirk, closely followed by the giant Carib, emerging from the jungle caught their first look at the last Don's plantation. With eager eyes they sought out the spot where the ancient castle had stood.

At a first startled glance Kirk cried out in dismay. Little wonder this, for where a noble edifice had stood a mournful sight now met their eyes. The magnificent, century old castle was now only a crumbled pile of broken timber, tumbled stone and crumbling mortar.

" Gone!" Kirk cried. "They are all gone!"

" It can't be as bad as that," said Pant. " At the first shock they would run from the house. Come on. Let's get down there."

No sooner said than done. Heedless of sharp stones that cut their shoes and sharper cacti that tore their flesh, they sprang away over the intervening space that lay between them and the tumbled pile of debris that had once been a very happy home.

It was with a cry of great joy that Kirk found his good friends, the family of the last Don, gathered upon a little circle of green that lay before the ruins.

After a quiet greeting befitting such a moment of great sadness, the boys took their places beside them.

It was a strange and moving sight that met their eyes as they looked about them. Even Pant, who had seen and experienced much, felt a choking sensation about his throat. Sprawled about upon the ground in various attitudes of sleep were the servants. Not so the family. The aged grandmother sat rocking gently back and forth. The last of the Dons, who had returned from a trip down the river just in time to see his home crumble to ruins, walked slowly before them. With hands clasped behind his back, he paced ceaselessly backward and forward in the moonlight.

Sitting beside the two ·boys, the dark-eyed Spanish girl, granddaughter of the last of the Dons, stared dreamily at the moon. To her no tragedy could be quite complete, for was she not young and beautiful? Was not all the world fresh and new? Strong she was, too, and brave. Many the jaguar that had known the steel of her unfaltering aim, many the wild turkey brought in by her to be roasted before the fire.

" Now," she said, and there was a note akin to joy in her tone, " we shall live like the savages in a house of thatched bamboo. Through the many cracks the morning sun shall peep at us as we awake. The rain shall fall gently upon our roof, the breeze shall play with my hair as I sit in our little castle of bamboo. The jaguar may look in upon us at night and the little wild pigs go grunting about our cabin. My good friend Kirk, and

my new friend Pant, we will live like savages
and life will be sweet for, after all, what is
so romantic as a little home in the midst of a
vast wilderness?"

Kirk smiled at her. He admired the courage of this child of an old, long lost race.

As for Pant, he scarcely heard her. He was
thinking of the fragments of a tale that had
come to his ears, the tale of the first Don and
his box of beaten silver filled with priceless
pearls.

"It may have been hidden in the walls of
that very building which the rude shock of
nature has wrecked," he told himself. "I
must have a look over those ruins.

"And then perhaps," he thought more
soberly still, "that may have been the box I
saw on the rocky ledge just as the earthquake shook the world down upon my head.
I wonder if that passage was closed? If it
is not, was the box buried in the wreckage?
Who can tell? I must know."

His thoughts returned to the American boy

who had accompanied him, who now sat close beside him. During the previous day he had been taken to the boy's room. There he had seen costly toilet articles, silver backed brushes, real tortoise shell combs, and genuine alligator skin traveling bags.

" He must belong to a rich family," he thought. " How then does he chance to be here so far from the home of other Americans, with only a black man as his companion? "

As if reading his thoughts, the other boy began to speak. " My uncle," he said, " has travelled much. He wishes me to know the world as he knows it. He is especially anxious for me to know much of Central America and her products. You see I am to be—" He paused, did not finish the sentence, stared away at the moon for a moment, then said quietly, as if the sentence he had not finished had really never been begun, " Uncle has had but one rule in all his travels: wherever a native, one who has always lived in the land he is visiting, will go, he will follow. That is the only rule he has laid down for me. My Carib is a native of this land. You saw how won‹ derfully he performed to-day."

Pant nodded.

"Wherever the Carib will go, I may follow."

A question leaped into Pant's mind, "Would the Carib venture again into the fear inspiring Maya cave?" He doubted it, yet he wished very much to return. He did not wish to go alone, had hoped that his new found friend might return with him. The story he heard that night as he sat before the ruins of that ancient home greatly strengthened his determination to revisit the cave.

No place could be better fitted for the telling of a tale of buccaneers and Spanish gold than that scene of ruins beneath the golden moon.

It was the last Don himself who told it. He told it all in Spanish, with many a dramatic gesture, but Kirk, who appeared to understand Spanish as well as he did his mother tongue, interpreted so skillfully that it seemed to Pant that the aged Don, with his venerable beard and coal black eyes, was telling the story directly to him.

And this was the tale he told:

Soon after gold had been brought to Europe from the New World and the rush for riches had begun, Ramon Salazar, who had amassed a comfortable fortune as a trader in old Madrid, but in whose veins coursed the spirit of the Crusaders, sold all his possessions and, having invested them in trade goods, sailed for America.

He landed on the east coast of Central America, but soon made his way over the difficult trail that led to the Pacific.

Ramon Salazar was a man of honor. He did not go in search of Aztec gold, nor did he lend aid to those shameful robberies of natives that still lie black on the pages of Spanish-American history.

Having made his way to the west coast, where he hoped to be forever safe from British and Scotch buccaneers, he set up a trading post and prospered.

Having learned of the rich pearl fisheries, he made a study of the matter and at last fitted out a schooner for the purpose of pearl fishing. Hiring divers and securing the protection of a Spanish man-of-war, he lingered long over those shallow waters whose submerged sandbars were rich with pearl bearing mussels.

He prospered again. Some pearls were sold, but the richest and choicest were kept in a box of beaten silver beneath the berth in his own stateroom. The room was not left unguarded night or day.

"Some bright morning," Ramon Salazar was fond of saying, " I shall take that box and sail away for sunny Spain. Then who cares what further riches the New World may still hold? But first," he always added, " I must have more pearls, larger pearls, a great pearl of pearls."

So he lingered, until one day a startling

thing happened. The east coast had long been infested by buccaneers. The west had been free. But now, out of a clear sky, one day as Ramon Salazar dined with the commander of the man-of-war, a boat load of marauders boarded the pearl fishing schooner, over-powered those on board, hoisted sail, and firing a shot across the bow of the man-of-war, they took to sea. And on board that schooner was Ramon Salazar's treasure of pearls.

"What sort of box was it that held the pearls?" Pant asked a bit breathlessly.

"Oh, my boy," was the old Don's reply, "that was long ago. Who can say? It was of beaten silver, perhaps as long as a man's forearm, and as thick as such a box should be."

"It might be the box," the boy thought to himself. "Surely I must return to the cave to-morrow."

"But to-morrow," he thought a moment later, "I cannot. There are other matters which must be attended to. I must not forget my grandfather, my photograph, and the chicle concession." He felt for the packet he had preserved so carefully. It was still safe.

"The bloody marauders did not succeed." The old Don's voice rose high pitched and shrill. "God confounded them. The man-of-war fired a shot that snapped their mainmast. They were captured. The treasure was restored.

"But my sire of many generations back fished for pearls no more. He took his box of pearls ashore. He did not return to Spain at once. Those were perilous times upon the sea. He would wait.

"He waited too long. Morgan came." The Don was fairly shouting now. "Morgan, the most bloodthirsty and cruel monster that ever sailed the Spanish Main. He came with many ships and two thousand men."

For a time after this he was silent. A first faint flush of light along the fringe of palms announced a new day.

"No," said the aged man, speaking more to himself than to them, "Morgan did not get the beaten silver box of pearls. Had he gotten it, one must have known. He was a great braggart.

"When my sire heard of Morgan's approach, he put the box under his arm and walked away into the jungle. He knew the jungle well. He could not have gotten lost in it. Yet he never returned. Somewhere—" He arose to fling his arms wide in a dramatic gesture, "somewhere in this jungle the box of beaten silver with the wealth of every Salazar within, lies hidden."

He resumed his seat. Light came more and more. Exhausted, the ancient Don fell asleep. But Pant stared at the dawn. He was thinking of the time when he might return to the Maya cave, and what he might find there when that day came.

And then, of a sudden, his thoughts took a fresh turn. He smiled as he thought of the strange code he had improvised at the spur of the moment before leaving his grandfather's office to plunge in the jungle, and the curious note he had left for Johnny Thompson. Had Johnny returned? Had he found the note? Had he been able to read it? What had kept Johnny so long? What was to happen? Were their paths that had run side by side so long to diverge at last?

Had he but known it, Johnny was at this moment planning a task which was to bring them close together, yet to keep them apart for many days to come. Such are the strange, wild chances of fate.

CHAPTER IX

CREEPING SHADOWS

Pant's wonderings about Johnny were not misplaced. To dismiss one's good pal from his mind is impossible. Johnny did not wish to forget Pant. He had discovered his note and found himself deeply concerned about it.

After leaving Don del Valle in Guatemala City, he took a train to the coast. There he caught a fruit boat to Stann Creek, and armed with a note from Don del Valle to his plantation manager ordering him to deliver twenty thousand bunches of bananas to the bearer, he reached Stann Creek just one hour before the train was to start up the narrow gauge railway to the Kennedy grapefruit plantation.

His first task was that of getting off a wireless message to Captain Jorgensen offering him a combined cargo of bananas and grapefruit for his return trip to the United States. With what feelings of hopes and fears he then awaited the good skipper's reply. Now he was elated by the hope that the *North Star* was still at his service, and now cast down by the fear that she was already loading mahogany, dyewood or cocoanuts.

He was not idle, however. Having gotten off his message, he hurried over to the office which Pant had left some hours before. It was with a deep feeling of unrest and disappointment that he found the place deserted. Colonel Longstreet had put the scattered papers to rights and repaired the damaged safe as best he could and he, too, had left. But on the table, weighted down by a polished square of ebony, was the curious note Pant had left. Scrawled across the top by the trembling hand of the old Colonel was Johnny's name.

" That was evidently intended for me," said Johnny, " but what in the name of all that's sane does it mean? "

" Some of Pant's doings," he grumbled as

with wrinkled brow he studied the miscellaneous jumble of figures, question marks and
trade signs. " Oh well, there's no time for
working puzzles now. I must get up the railway to Kennedy's fruit farm. Won't they be
joyous!" With that he thrust the paper in
his pocket, but it was not entirely forgotten.

He was in the curious day coach with its
seats along the sides and its broad open spaces
in lieu of windows, waiting for the train to
start, when he opened Captain Jorgensen's
wireless message.

His fingers trembled, his face grew sober as
he unfolded the bit of yellow paper.

" What if—

" But no!" With a quick exclamation of
joy, he read:

" *Congratulations. The North Star awaits
your order.*"

" Couldn't be better," was the way the boy
expressed it as he walked among the gold
laden fruit trees two hours later. He was
talking to Madge Kennedy. No wall flower,

this girl. Sun-browned arms, honest freckles, strong and healthy muscles, that was Madge Kennedy. Though only nineteen years of age, she had taken over the largest share of the task of keeping the orchard in order.

Underbrush and creepers grow fast in this warm, moist land. A constant war must be waged against them. Johnny had found her doing her bit by swinging a short stout brush scythe. Two husky Carib Indians were working with her, but Johnny noted with no little pleasure that she was the best worker of the three.

After taking the scythe and finishing the swath, he dropped beside her in the evening shade, and told her of his success.

"It's your grandfather's chance, and yours," he said with enthusiasm. "Think of it! Five thousand boxes of grapefruit. That many at least. And we'll get the top price. America has never tasted such fruit. Your grandfather has the boxes ready to set up?"

She nodded.

"Then there's nothing to stop us. Your grandfather can find men to pick and pack the fruit?"

"Carib Indians," she said in quiet confidence, "hundreds of them, thousands if necessary. They love grandfather, every last one of them.

"Do you know, my friend," her voice was husky, "my grandfather is a sort of second Livingston. Livingston went to Africa. Grandfather came to Central America. He has been all over it. There is no dark little spot in any tiny republic where he has not been. He has visited Maya Indians who were supposed to kill a white man at sight. They did not touch him. Love, sympathy and a simple modesty are the charms that protect him. There's not a family within the district he has not helped in time of trouble. There is always plenty of trouble. Oh yes, he can find the men; without pay if necessary."

"It won't be necessary. Do you know how much five thousand acres of the finest grape-

fruit in the world will bring in New York?"
She shook her head.

"Neither do I. Thousands of dollars, there's no question. Then your grandfather and you can leave this wilderness."

"Leave—leave it?"

The girl's eyes swept the scene before her. In the immediate foreground all green and gold was the orchard; beyond that a broad stretch of green where an occasional cohune nut palm with leaves thirty feet long broke the even green. Back of all that, nestling against the vast, impenetrable jungle, was the long, low house.

"Leave it?" she repeated. "Grandfather would not leave it. He loves the land and his black Caribs too well.

"He left it once." Her voice grew husky again. "War. He left then. He was gone three years. They made him a captain. They say it was uncanny the way he led his men, his black Caribs from Central America, and how in every bloody battle he escaped unharmed." She was silent for a moment. The shadows deepened.

"Do you know," she went on softly, "he never speaks of it now. And he never allows anyone to call him Captain Kennedy. That's what he was, you know. But somehow I love him a lot more for it."

"He's got company!" she exclaimed, springing up and shaking herself as if to break a spell that had come over her. "One of those dark Spaniards. I don't like him. Br-r-r-r! He makes me think of the wolf in Little Red Riding Hood. But we must go in. It isn't respectable not to. He's been talking some sort of business, but must be through by now."

"Business?" Johnny had the question on his lips, but did not ask it. He was destined in good time to know what sort of business that was, and to get little enough comfort from the knowledge.

They found Kennedy sitting alone on the veranda.

"How do you do, Mr. Kennedy," said Johnny, putting out his hand. "Congratulate me. I have my cargo completed. Bananas. You may begin packing your fruit to-morrow. It will be in New York within ten days if we have luck. We—"

He broke short off. A tall Spaniard had emerged from the shadows. He had heard all, and the black cloud on his face was not all due to his dark Spanish skin.

He did not speak to the boy, but turning to Kennedy bade him good-night, then strode rapidly away to the spot where his saddle horse was tethered.

It was astonishing, the effect of this man upon Johnny's spirits. It was as if threatening shadows had begun to crawl upon him.

"Bah!" he whispered to himself. "Probably never see him again."

In this he was wrong. He was destined to see him many times, in fact to see him the very next day, and to get a decided shock from the encounter.

"Business," he whispered to himself.

"What sort of business?" He thought of Madge Kennedy and the Spaniard, then dismissed them from his mind.

"Sit here with grandfather," he heard the girl saying. "I'll have some food ready in a jiffy."

Mechanically he sat down, and as he did so, discovered that the sudden night of the jungle had blotted out every track of the orchard, the wide spreading green and the dark forest that lay beyond.

CHAPTER X

CAMP SMOKE

While searching among the ruins of the old Don's castle early that morning, Pant found an ancient field glass that had by some chance escaped destruction. A clumsy model it was, and of such ancient design that it might well have been a present from Queen Isabella to Columbus. It was a powerful one, for all that, and would serve his purpose well. The old Don readily consented to loaning it.

With this new treasure in his pack, Pant struck off toward the hills. He had gone a short distance when disturbing thoughts came to him.

"Something may happen to my film," he told himself. "I must not forget."

Not willing to depend entirely upon memory, he took sheets of paper from his pack and stuck four of them together with the sticky juice of a wild vine. Painstakingly he traced as well as he could the outlines of his grandfather's concessions and of the rival companies, as shown by the film. Having done this, he rebound his pack and continued on his upward journey.

" Soon," he thought as he traveled on, " perhaps to-morrow, we may begin operations." He had a glorious mental picture of the light on his grandfather's face as he saw a hundred Caribs at work on their concession and saw in it a promise of a rebuilt fortune.

" Chicle gathering," he thought. " What a strange way to amass a fortune! Yet how sure."

As he closed his eyes he saw the work begun. The Carib Indians—great bronze men, one time cannibals, now partially Christianized and caught in the spell of white man's influence, had always been friends of his grandfather, as they had been of Kennedy and of every true man.

" The old Colonel will appeal to them," he thought to himself. " They will respond. They will flock to his banner. A hundred, two hundred strong, shouldering axes and machetes, they'll march into the jungle."

He had a mental vision of what would follow. In the heart of the jungle a camp site would be chosen. Palms would be felled, rude shelters would be formed. After this the real work would begin. Scattering out through the jungle, the Caribs would search out the largest, most promising sapodilla trees. These, by the aid of their bare toes and a single strap, they would scale to a distance of thirty or forty feet. Beginning at the top, working their way round and round the trunk, they would cut in the bark a spiral groove reaching to the ground. Down the groove sap from the bark would ooze. When a sufficient quantity had reached the canvas sack placed at the bottom of the groove, it would be collected and carried to camp where, in a huge copper kettle over a great fire that blazed merrily, the sap would be boiled down.

When the chicle had cooled, it would be kneaded like bread dough until it was thick enough to form in cakes. Then it would be poured into moulds and allowed to harden.

After that, packed two cakes in a gunny-sack, it would be carried on Caribs' backs to the nearest stream. By pit-pan to the sea, then by sailing schooner to the nearest shipping point, Belize.

" And then," he sighed, " our work is done. The Central Chicle Company will take it off our hands. They are the real exporters."

His heart warmed as he saw the long rows of black and brown men and seemed to catch their wierd chant as they marched on the first lap of the long journey with the freshly gathered chicle on their backs.

" We will succeed," he told himself. " We must ! "

One other thought came to him at that moment, a rather vexing thought. He would return to the Maya cave. Sooner or later he would go back and enter in search of the mysterious metal box he had seen there.

" And if I should find the beaten silver box," he said to himself, " if the pearls should still be within, after all these years, to whom would they belong? "

" Finders keepers," an old adage, kept running through his mind. Yet this did not quite satisfy him. This problem was soon dismissed from his mind. He had business before him.

He had reached the rocky crest of the hill that lay at the back of the old Don's pasture. From this promontory one might command a view of the valley below and might trace the course of its main stream, the Rio de Grande, for a distance of thirty miles.

Hardly had he reached this observation post and spread his crude map out before him, than the. smoke of a score of campfires rose lazily up from the jungle valley some ten miles away.

" That's well within our territory," he said

with a start and an exclamation of anger. " That's Diaz. He has already begun operations on our trees. He is very bold. He takes too much for granted. But we—we'll show him! " He clenched his fists hard.

But what was this? Off to the right, scarcely three miles distant, a second smoke rose above the tree tops.

" Who can that be? " he asked himself. At once his mind was in a whirl. That it was not a second group of Diaz's men he knew well enough. Men in the jungle always huddle in one group. Perhaps it is fear of that unknown peril that lurks in the jungle that causes them to do this. Who can say? Enough that this is a custom of the land.

" Can it be that the Central Chicle Company is also poaching on our ground? " he asked himself. " It does not seem possible. And yet, who else can it be?

" I must know," he resolved. " I will see." At that, following the bed of a stream, he struck boldly down through the jungle toward the spot where the first camp site smoke still rose.

For two hours he fought the jungle. Scrambling down a water drenched ledge, battling the clinging bramble, creeping low beneath a growth of palms, and racing down the trunk of a massive fallen mahogany tree, he forced his way forward until he found himself on a steep ledge looking upon the winding sweep of the river.

Here he paused to stare in astonishment. Less than a year before a mahogany company had logged a wide strip next to the river. The jungle had not yet retaken the clearing. In the midst of this cleared space, some hundreds of yards apart, stood two bands of men. Axes flashed from their shoulders. Here and there the two foot blade of a machete gleamed.

" It—why it's as if they were lined up for battle! Who can they be? " The boy's breath came short and quick. He took the old field glass from his pack and focused it upon the two groups of men.

The band over to the right were of mixed lineage, some Spaniards, some half-castes, some blacks. He could guess this from their postures and the garments they wore.

"Diaz," was his mental comment. "But the others?"

A tall, thin man, wearing a khaki suit and a helmet, stood out before the others. Unquestionably he was a white man.

"But the others are Caribs." A thrill shot up the boy's spine. The distance was great. At that distance it was difficult to tell, and yet—

His field glass was now riveted upon the white man in the khaki suit. He was evidently speaking to a leader of the other group.

"It can't be!" The boy's throat tightened. "And yet—and yet—" The white man threw up his arms in a gesture of impatience. There was no mistaking that gesture.

"Grandfather, the old Colonel!" The cry stuck in the boy's throat. What was he saying? The distance was too great to hear.

As the boy stood there silent, watching, his knees trembled and his head whirled. The thing that had happened was evident. Having grown impatient waiting for Pant's return, the old Colonel had gotten together a band of Carib chicleros and had gone into the jungle to gather from the narrow stretch of land which he knew to be his. He had happened to stop near the crafty Spaniard's illegal camp. The two bands had met.

" And now," the boy told himself with a shudder, " there will be a fight."

A fight? What did that mean? Certainly terrible bloodshed. Between this half-caste band and the Caribs there had always been waged a sort of gorilla warfare. Now here they were face to face, a hundred men on either side. Armed with axes, machetes and revolvers, they would do terrible execution. It would be a battle to the death.

" I must get down there. I have the picture of the map," the boy told himself. " That may help. I must be beside the old colonel."

He paused for a moment's thought as to how the affair was likely to end. A mile of tangled brush lay between him and them. Could he reach the spot in time?

As if to answer his question, the white and brown line, Diaz's men, suddenly began marching straight on toward the lone white man who stood out before the Caribs.

" Too late! " The boy all but sank upon the ground. Yet, getting a better hold upon himself, he stood there wide-eyed and terrified.

Never had he witnessed a thing so strikingly dramatic as the deadly regular march of those men. And never had he seen anything so heroic as the image of the aged colonel standing there erect, silent, motionless, facing them all.

Sixty seconds passed. the men had covered half the distance. Ninety seconds; they were very near. A hundred; they were all but upon the silent figure. Still with arms hanging motionless, he stood there. It was a tense moment. The boy ceased breathing. Standing there, leaning far forward, he thought a prayer, that was all.

But what was this? At some call from the side, all faces turned right. The marching column broke step, then came to a dead halt. As they did so, erect, with head held high, a stately figure rode in before them.

" The old Don, the last of the Dons! " Pant breathed. " How strange! "

To all appearance the aged Spaniard began to speak. The others paused to listen.

" Now—now is my chance! " The boy's mind worked like a spring lock. " I may make it yet." At once he dropped over the ledge and made his way down the perilous cliff until at last he reached the tangled mass of vegetation that lay at the foot of the rocky ledge.

Battling now with all his might, heedless of brambles that tore at his clothing, of stinging palm leaves that cut his face, and the ooze of the lowlands that threatened to engulf him, expecting every moment to hear the war cry of the Caribs, he fought his way through.

He will never know what the aged Don said to the Spaniard, Diaz, and his mixed band of chicleros, yet he will never think of the Don and his speech without experiencing anew a deep feeling of gratitude. For it was that speech which, beyond a shadow of a doubt, saved his grandfather's life. Had the fight ever begun he would have been the first to fall, for he was well in advance of his men, and was not the man to turn his back to the enemy.

As it was, when puffing, perspiring, bleeding from wounds inflicted by the jungle, the boy burst into the clearing, he found the aged nobleman, the last of the Dons, speaking calmly to the men and the men of both camps as calmly listening.

What was there about this aged Spaniard to inspire such calm? Was it his venerable appearance? Was it that he was of noble birth? Who can say? So intent were the men upon his words that Pant was able to slip unobserved to the old colonel's side and to explain in a few well chosen words just what the film he held in his hand meant to them.

His grandfather's face lighted with a smile not soon to be forgotten. He spoke quietly to his foreman:

" Tell the men to withdraw after the speech. There will be no fighting, no fight, do you understand? We have found a better way."

Word was quickly passed down the line. The loyal Caribs stood ready to obey.

As the old Don ended his speech with a bow of his venerable head, Pant pressed forward to grip his hand.

" We will never forget." He repeated the words in Spanish. " Never forget."

The aged Spaniard bowed and smiled.

A moment later Colonel Longstreet was speaking to the crafty Diaz. His words were few and well chosen. He would withdraw his men if need be. There would be no fight. He, Diaz, might gather all the chicle he chose to in that valley. One thing he must remember, however; the real owner of the concession was in possession of an exact reproduction of the stolen map. Not alone that, but he had positive proof that he, Diaz, stole the map.

" Positive proof! " he repeated. " And remember, the profit on every pound of chicle you gather on our territory must be paid to us. The law of the land is just." With these words he walked away.

No smoke arose next morning over the spot where Diaz's camp had stood. Diaz and his men had returned to their own narrow boundaries. Yet Diaz was not through contesting the rights of an American to gather chicle on the upper reaches of the Rio de Grande. He had lost one battle, but others were to follow.

There had been rain during a previous night. Now, as if to prove that nature and the fates were on the side of Pant and his recently discovered grandfather, there came a perfect deluge of rain. Rain is indispensable to chicle gathering. Now the work could go forward at once.

CHAPTER XI

BATTLING AGAINST ODDS

In the meantime Johnny Thompson was allowing no grass to grow under his feet. Having arranged with Kennedy to put his fruit on the wharf within five days, he secured the services of a wheezy but dependable motor boat and started at once to Porte Zalaya, the headquarters of Don del Valle's banana growing company.

He arrived at three o'clock that afternoon, and went at once to the long low office building at the end of the wharf. There he asked for Armacito Diaz, the manager.

Johnny did not know that Armacito Diaz was the same Spaniard who had been doing his utmost to defeat Pant in his work of rebuilding his grandfather's fortune. For reasons best known to himself, though possessed of concessions of his own, Diaz played the part of a humble servant under the employ of Don del Valle's direction. He was the same man who had given Johnny the black look at Kennedy's. Since the valley of the Rio de Grande was only a short distance off, he had ridden to his chicle camp, there to meet temporary defeat in his attempt at looting the old colonel's concessions. Fox-like, he was now in his den behind clouded glass walls, administering the affairs of the banana planter.

A dapper Spanish clerk took Johnny's message, then disappeared through a door at the back.

"He will see you in a minute," said the polite clerk.

Johnny sat down on a bench to wait. The day was warm. There was no breeze. The bench was hard. The minute grew into a half hour, an hour.

Johnny rose to inquire patiently regarding the impending interview.

"One minute." The clerk was gone.

"One minute. Just one more minute and he will see you."

Another hour passed, a precious hour to Johnny. He rose once more; but this time, ignoring the clerk, he threw back the swinging gate, strode across the narrow enclosure, threw open the door at the rear and entered the room beyond.

Imagine the surprise and shock that awaited him when he found himself face to face with the frowning Spaniard of the previous night, the man Madge Kennedy had said was like the wolf in Little Red Riding Hood.

The man sprang from his chair.

"Senor Diaz?" said Johnny in as easy a tone as he could command.

"You intrude," said the other without answering his question.

"If you are Armacito Diaz," said Johnny, looking him square in the eye, "I have a right to intrude. I have a message from your master. You have delayed its delivery unnecessarily."

To himself Johnny was saying, " This man Diaz? Here is a nice mess. He already dislikes me for some reason or another. Perhaps I am in his way somehow. Perhaps, like many Spaniards, he hates all Americans. However that may be, he will do his master's bidding."

" What's this? " The frown on the Spaniard's brow deepened as he read the message Johnny laid before him. " Gather twenty thousand defective bunches for shipment? What nonsense! "

" So you are Diaz? "

" I am Diaz. And you? "

" Johnny Thompson."

" American." There was contempt in the man's tone. " Adventurer! "

" American," said Johnny quietly. " As for the other, it matters little to you whether I am or not. You will deliver the bananas at the dock, this dock, to-morrow morning; at Dock No. 2 the next day; and at No. 3 that same night."

" The order is forged," said the manager, throwing the letter on the table. " My master would have no part in such nonsense. Twenty thousand defective bunches!"

" Six hand bunches," corrected Johnny quietly. " The order is not forged. You know it is not. Ignore it at your own risk. Your position as manager is at stake. You will send your men into the field at once."

" *Manana.* To-morrow," said the manager after several moments spent in thought.

" To-day," said Johnny.

" It is impossible. The men are scattered. We have on hand no more loading for ten days."

" All right, then to-morrow. To-morrow evening we will be at this dock ready to load. We can load at night."

To this the Spaniard made no answer. After waiting a respectable time for a reply, Johnny left the office.

As he walked out into the warm tropical sunshine his head was in a whirl. The feeling of dark shadows creeping up from behind him was so strong that he involuntarily turned to look back. There was no one.. The dusty street was empty.

"Strange," he thought, "that he should seem to hate me and want to thwart my plans. He seems to be a friend of Kennedy. He must know I am working only for Kennedy's good. Why then should he behave as he does?"

He was destined to ask that question many times before he discovered the real answer.

Just then as he thrust his hand deep in his pocket, a habit he had when engrossed in thought, he felt a crumpled bit of paper.

"Pant's message," he said to himself as he drew it forth.

"Wonder what it's all about?" His brow wrinkled in puzzled thought. "Wish I knew. Wish I had the key to it. It might mean a lot. Wish I knew where he is, and what's happening to him."

Finding a grassy spot in the shadow of the dock, he sat puzzling over that jumble of figures and signs which he felt sure was meant to convey an important message to him, but which in reality meant nothing to him.

" The key! " he exclaimed at last in disgust. " If only I had the key to it! "

The key to this riddle, if only he could have known it, lay back there in the little bamboo office where Pant had left the note. He had expected Johnny to sit right down beside the portable typewriter and study out the meaning of his strange cipher message.

As it happened, there had not been time for this; a great pity, too, for the message was an important one. Its solving at that moment might have saved Johnny many a heartache. Without the typewriter, however, it was going to be difficult, very difficult indeed. In the end he pocketed the message still unread.

* * * * *

There is only one silence more complete than the silence of the jungle at mid-day. That is the silence to be experienced at the heart of a great banana plantation in the heat of the day. There not a twig drops but its fall is heard. The march of a thousand ants going and coming over their tiny paths gives forth as definite and distinct a sound as the tramp of an army.

Johnny was hearing and watching these toiling ants. He got scant comfort from these observations. Their actions reminded him of three days of painful failure. The *North Star* was at loading dock No. 1, had been for three days, yet her hold was as empty as the day she had tied up there. There were no bananas at the dock.

" Here there are plenty," Johnny told himself, glancing up at the three great bunches that hung directly over his head, and away at hundreds on every hand.

Again his attention was drawn by the rustle of rushing ants.

" How strange," he thought. " It would take a million of these ants to weigh as much as I do, yet they are getting on with the thing they wish done. I have failed."

He started. The thing the ants were doing was quite like the work he wished to do. They were tearing bits of leaves from a vine and were carrying them away beneath the ground.

" Just as a hundred men should be carrying bunches of bananas to our ship," he thought.

" Yes, we have no bananas," he grinned in spite of himself. All about him were bananas, a vast unending sea of them, a hundred thousand bunches. He had been promised twenty thousand. That treacherous Spanish manager, Diaz, had blocked his every move. Not a bunch had he delivered.

" *Manana! Manana!* " He had whispered over and over. " My workmen are scattered. They have gone turtle hunting. They are not here. To-morrow they will be back. To-morrow. To-morrow."

" To-morrow! " the boy exclaimed. " When I get back to the States I shall have that word removed from the dictionary."

Suddenly his lips parted, but no sound came

forth. Rising upon one knee, he crouched there poised like some wild creature ready for a spring.

"Was that a voice?"

He felt reasonably sure of it, yet in this land of monkeys, parrots and mocking birds one could never be quite sure.

"If it is," he told himself, "if they are that crafty Spaniard's men sent to hunt me down, there may be a fight.

"And yet," he thought, "why should he wish to hunt me down, to have me killed? He's having his own sweet way. What more could he wish?"

He thought of the man sitting there on the veranda with Kennedy, thought too of Madge Kennedy. Madge Kennedy of the golden hair and frank freckled face, the bright, alert, clean Scotch girl of the jungle, and for some reason or another his brow clouded.

"If it's a fight they want," he said, clenching his fists tight, "they're quite welcome to it, though I'd be the last to start it."

Having caught no further sound, he settled back to his task of watching the ants stowing away bits of leaves, and of thinking over his own problems.

" It's as if they were hurrying through with an important task," he told himself, watching the tiny workers with renewed interest, "as if they were preparing for some great change, perhaps some gigantic natural catastrophe, an earthquake, a storm, a—

" I wonder — " his brow wrinkled as he gazed away toward the western sky. But no, there were no clouds, only a faint haze that spread over all the sky, faintly obscuring the sun.

" Nothing much I guess. Getting superstitious," he told himself. "Must be going back. But not just yet."

He had come to the heart of this banana plantation for two reasons. He had wanted to carry on a little investigation of his own, and to think his problems through.

The investigation had confirmed his suspi-

cions. There were no workmen in this field.
Diaz had said there were fifty men here gathering bananas. He had promised that the
fruit would be at the dock, a train load of it
next morning.

"A plain out-and-out lie!" Johnny told
himself bitterly. "He knows he has me defeated. Any untruth will do. To-morrow my
option on the *North Star* expires. Then she
will steam away. After that Kennedy's grapefruit may rot on the dock. He will be worse
off than before. His Caribs have gathered and
packed the fruit and there will be no money
to pay them. What a blunderer I am!"

It was all quite true. The sleek, soft spoken
Spanish manager of the plantation had, after
that first stormy meeting, seemed to suddenly
become quite friendly. He had invited Johnny
to lunch and had feasted him quite royally.
He had promised that his men who were out
setting nets for turtles would be called in.
Johnny should dock his ship. The bananas
would be ready next evening.

That had been the first day. At the end of the second day no bananas had appeared. Johnny had sought out the Spaniard. He had treated the boy to a sumptuous dinner and had assured him that to-morrow the men would go for bananas. *"Manana, manana,"* he had repeated, wringing the boy's hand.

If only Johnny had been able to read Pant's note! But he had not.

Captain Jorgensen had waited patiently for three days; then, having been offered a cargo of chicle and cocoanuts in Belize, he had given Johnny notice that if bananas were not coming aboard by the evening of the next day, his option would expire and he would be obliged to steam away.

He had said all this in the kindest tone possible. He liked Johnny. He liked Kennedy and his granddaughter, and would do anything within his power, but the company that owned his ship would stand for no further delay.

"It's all right, quite all right. Very fine,

Senor, very fine," Diaz had said when, in despair, Johnny had sought him out once more.
" To-day my men are among the bananas. To-
morrow morning you shall have a train load."

Johnny had doubted his word. He had
trudged away up the narrow gauge railway
track to see. He had tramped for miles in the
shade of great spreading banana plants and
had not seen a workman.

" They are not here, will not be here. We
will have no bananas. Tomorrow the *North
Star* sails away. My plan fails. I have been
worse than useless to my friends.

" And yet," he said doggedly, " there must
be some way out. There must!"

Again his eyes followed the long proces-
sion of ants. Once more he glanced toward
the sky. The veil over the sun had grown a
shade deeper.

" They are hurrying faster than ever," he
said as he again watched the interesting pro-
cession. " It is as if—"

Once more his thoughts broke short off.

This time from just behind the second row of banana plants he felt sure he had caught the low murmur of voices.

Strangely enough, at this moment when he crouched there, nerves tense, eyes and ears alert, watching for the mysterious unknown ones, there flashed before his mind the picture of a short stout white man standing at the foot of a dock. He had seen that man only the day before.

There was a mystery about that man. Who was he? Whence had he come and how? No steamers had arrived from the States. Yet he was unmistakably American. His clothes were well tailored. He had the air of one who is prosperous and who finds himself often in a position of authority. What could be his business in Central America?

The first time Johnny had seen him he had been standing at the foot of the dock.

" For all the world as if some strange magic had sent him, bone dry and all spick and span right up out of the sea," the boy told himself.

This mysterious American had gone directly to the office of Diaz. When he left that office a half hour later Diaz had accompanied him as far as the door. There had been a smile on the crafty Spaniard's face; not the sort of smile one loves to see.

"That smile," Johnny now told himself, "should have been enough to warn me."

There was a rumor afloat that the prosperous looking American was some high official of the Fruit Company.

"If that is true, he may be behind my defeat," he told himself. "But one never can tell. I—"

He paused. His heart skipped a beat. From close at hand there sounded a heavy footstep.

"Diaz's men," he thought, slipping his machete half out of its scabbard. "They'll find I can fight if that must be."

The next instant a figure loomed before him, a great black giant with the face of a south sea cannibal, and a smile—well, such a smile as one sees only in tropical lands.

As the man saw Johnny, he turned half about to speak to some one behind him. The language he used was strange to the boy.

" Two of them," he thought.

But somehow his fear was gone. That smile was disarming. The next instant Johnny smiled. He laughed out loud, then leaped to his feet to stretch forth both hands in greeting. For the person who moved up to a position beside the towering black Indian was none other than Madge Kennedy.

" How, how did you find me? " Johnny exclaimed when greetings had been exchanged.

Madge turned to the Carib. " These people who have lived here always know everything. He brought me here. But why did you hide? "

" I didn't, exactly. I came here to get the truth. Having gotten it, I remained to digest it? "

" Did you enjoy it? "

" Not exactly." His tone was dubious. " I suppose you know I've played my last card, and lost? "

" I—I guessed it. I'm sorry."

The girl's tone was deep and mellow, like the low note of a cello.

" So am I," said Johnny, " but only sorry for **you**, you and your wonderful old grandfather."

" For us? " She let forth a merry little laugh. " We shall get on, one way or another. One always does down here you know."

" It is rather bad, though," she admitted, sitting down upon the ground. " You see—"

She paused to glance away at the sun. Where the sun should have been, there was no sun, only a dull, veiled sky. Her brow wrinkled, but she did not comment upon it.

" It is bad," she went on. " We may have to sell the orchard."

" Sell the orchard! " Johnny was surprised. " To whom? "

" Diaz." She leaned far forward as she answered. " He wishes to buy it. That was what he and grandfather were talking about when you came the other night."

" Diaz! " Johnny took in a long breath.

The picture of the stout, prosperous American and the crafty Spaniard passed before him. " So that's his game," he thought. " He's got Kennedy in a hole. The sale of his grapefruit would let him out. Diaz is determined to block the shipment, and is in the position to do it. The scoundrel! "

" The Spaniards down here don't love us, the English and Scotch, too much," Madge Kennedy went on. " The trouble goes clear back to the days of buccaneers and the Spanish Main. The English and Scotch logwood gatherers drove the Spaniards from the mouth of the Belize River. They have never forgiven us.

" Oh yes," she laughed, " they trade with us when there is a profit to be made, but after all their knife is always near our throats. Diaz thinks he has us and he means to do his worst.

" I suppose," she said, " we'll have to sell to the Spaniards. It will break grandfather's heart. He wouldn't mind if it went to a fellow countryman.

"You know," she reminisced, "that's been our land longer than I can remember, much longer. It's our home. Don't you see, Johnny? It's the only home I've ever known. You don't like to see your home sold to some one you don't like, do you? Your home is part of you. When you sell it, you sell part of yourself.

"It would have been all right if it hadn't been for the Panama disease. Our land was all in bananas then, and grandfather was getting rich. We had bananas like these." She spread her arms wide. "Better than these. Then the disease came. Plants wilted like flowers before a hot wind. It wasn't long before there were no bananas. Along the Stann Creek railroad they used to gather twenty-five thousand bunches a week. Now they don't get twenty-five hundred." She sighed.

"Grandfather was cheerful even then. He always will be. He's a sport, a great big good sport with a soul." The tones of her voice grew mellow and deep.

"He planted grapefruit. You know the rest. And now, now I guess we—" Her voice broke. "I guess we're done."

Suddenly Johnny sprang to his feet. There came a roar as of rushing water.

"Look! Only look!" There was awe in Johnny's voice.

Madge turned pale. The top of a palm tree, left for some unknown reason to grow among the bananas, was writhing and twisting as if in mortal agony.

At the same instant the entire broad sweep of banana plants moved forward to bow low as if in obeisance to some god and, caught by a terrific onrush of air, the three of them, Johnny, Madge Kennedy and the Indian, were thrown in a heap against a stump.

Madge scrambled to her knees, rubbed her eyes, stared away at the sky, then said in a tense, scarcely audible whisper:

"May God protect us! It is to be a tornado!"

CHAPTER XII

DESTRUCTION

Banana land is never fully cleared before planting. Great giants of the forest, mahogany, nargusta, black tamarind, Santa Maria, and many other great trees are girdled and left standing to rattle their dry and leafless limbs like bones on a gibbet to every wind that blows. In the time of a great wind such as often sweeps across the Caribbean Sea, dead limbs of girdled trees and the ponderous fronds of palms come crashing down upon the less stalwart banana plants.

It was on such a half cleared plantation that Johnny Thompson, Madge Kennedy and the giant black Carib Indian found themselves when the storm came tearing in from the sea.

That they were in a tight place Johnny knew right well. He had heard of these tropical storms. Many an old timer had told him of braving them upon sea and land. Travelers in this land are told in awed tones strange tales of terrific gales.

Johnny shuddered as he heard the crack and crash of giant trees torn and tortured by the wind.

" What shall we do? " he said to the girl. " Can we get out of this? "

" No." She spoke slowly, deliberately, as one may who knows her land and its storms. " The tossing banana plants will shut off the roads. Some will fall, blocking the way. The wind will increase in violence. The storm will last for hours."

" Then we must find shelter."

" Yes."

" But where? "

The girl shook her head. " I don't know."

As if determined to destroy them, the palm sent a second discarded frond sailing toward them. It fell with a crash that brought down a dozen banana plants with it.

Madge shuddered.

The currents of winds above them seemed greater than those that agitated the banana plants just over their heads. Great dead trees writhed and tossed as if in terrible agony, while from here and there at a distance there came the crash of one that had been broken off or uprooted.

Of a sudden the force of the winds appeared to double in volume. At the same instant Johnny saw a great black mass come leaping toward him. Powerless to move or speak for a second, he saw the thing leap straight at him. Giving up hope, he shut his eyes.

There came a deafening crash. A sharp quick cut across the face brought him to himself. He leaped to his feet. The wind caught him and threw him violently. His senses reeled. The thing was too monstrous. What had happened? His face was bleeding. He did not feel it. His senses were benumbed.

"I must act!" he told himself savagely. "Something must be done. There is the girl."

He had succeeded in coming back into control of his senses when something hurtled past him.

"It's the Carib," he told himself. "No, the girl!" He had caught the flash of her blue dress.

"It is the Carib and the girl." He realized that the aged black giant had seized the girl in his arms and was battling his way straight into the teeth of the storm.

"What can he hope to do?" he asked himself as, first on hands and knees, then crouching low, on his feet, he struggled forward in their wake.

Dimly, he became conscious of the thing that had happened. A great sapodillo tree, uprooted by the storm, had pitched straight at them.

"Ten feet nearer and we would have been killed," he thought. "That's the black bulk that leaped at us."

The thing the Carib was doing puzzled him. He was fighting his way over broken branches

and beneath threatening trees. At last, finding himself at a branchless trunk, and seeing
his way blocked by a tangled mass of vegetation, he held the girl in one arm while, ape-
like, he climbed to the prostrate trunk, then
against the terrific force of the gale battled his
way to the shelter of the roots of the giant
tree.

" What strength ! " thought Johnny. " What
magnificent power ! "

He was content to creep the length of the
log, to come up panting beside them. Not a
word was said. The din about them was deafening. The howl of the wind, the crash of
breaking, falling limbs, the groan of tortured
trees, all this was enough to inspire silent awe.

A moment they rested here. A moment
only. Then, at the Carib's sign, they slid off
the log to battle their way around the up-ended
roots.

Johnny saw the Carib suddenly disappear.
He saw a chasm yawning before him; saw the
girl leap. He followed her, landing with a

shock that set his teeth rattling, then became conscious of the fact that the storm was not cracking about his ears.

"Storm cellar provided by nature," he thought. It was true. The chasm left by the tree roots was ten feet deep.

"Gabriel thought of it," said Madge. "It is his country. He is very old. He always knows the right thing to do. Isn't it grand?"

Johnny thought it a little more than grand.

"We British and you Americans," she said slowly, "think we are very smart. We know many things. But the natives of other lands, they know many useful things that we never dreamed of.

"But you are hurt. Your face—it is bloody." Her eyes grew suddenly large.

"No, I guess not. Nothing much. It must have been the branch of that fallen tree. Lucky it didn't kill us all."

The wound, little more than a deep scratch, was soon dressed. Then, against the sheltered side of the "storm cellar" left by the tree roots, they sat down to patiently await the passing of the storm.

" Getting worse. Listen! " Johnny whispered as the wind whipped the dead branches with increasing fury.

The girl shuddered. " The bananas," she said. " They will all be down. Ruined. The whole plantation. There will be no more for nine months."

" Then it's the end of our plans."

" I am afraid so."

" Anyway, Diaz had us blocked."

" Perhaps."

" Did you ever think," the girl said after a while, " that even had you succeeded in loading the bananas and grapefruit you might have been worse off than before? "

" Why? The ship's all right. Isn't she? "

" Yes, but at the other end? Did you never think that an organization like the Fruit Company, powerful enough to control the purchasing of all fruit of Central America, could control the selling market as well. Do you think

a big commission merchant would dare purchase your load of bananas and grapefruit?
Could you deliver to him regularly? You
couldn't. What could he do if the powerful
Fruit Company should refuse to sell to him
because he bought from you? Not a thing."

Johnny was stunned. He had not thought
of this.

"So you see," said the girl in a very quiet
tone, "while it was brave and generous of you
to try to help grandfather and—and me, after
all it was just as well that nature and Spanish
trickery took a hand."

"I'm not so sure," said Johnny grimly. "I'd
like to have the chance at it, even now. I'd
risk it. I—why, I'd hunt up my old friend
Tony, the push-cart man, if necessary, and
I'd say, 'Tony, I have a ship load of fruit at
half price down at the dock. Go tell your pals.'

"In a half hour's time there would be a mile
of push-carts coming my way.

"But now," he said slowly, almost despon-
dently, "this is the end."

In this he was mistaken. It was scarcely the beginning of what was to prove a thrilling adventure. "The *North Star!*" he exclaimed suddenly. "She was tied to the dock. What will happen to her?"

Since the girl did not know the answer, she did not reply.

A moment later, the Carib crept up the bank of the pit to disappear into the storm. Ten minutes later, when he reappeared, his jacket was filled with cocoanuts.

"Food and drink," smiled Madge. "We shall not fare so badly in our cave, after all."

Still the wind raged on. Rain came and with it night.

A great flat boulder, turned half over by the uprooted tree, left a sort of narrow grotto with a stone floor. By crowding well back into this grotto, Johnny and the girl were able to escape the terrific downpour of rain. The Carib, who minded a wetting about as much as a duck, sat chuckling to himself beneath the tree's great roots.

For a time the girl and the boy talked of many things, of their homes, of their native lands, of strange customs and stranger laws, of the sea and of the land.

The conversation turned to chicle gathering. Then it was that Johnny told of his friend Pant, how he had found his long lost grandfather and how they were, beyond doubt, at that very moment gathering chicle in the forest around Rio de Grande.

"The Rio de Grande!" exclaimed the girl. "Diaz gathers chicle there. He will stop them if he can."

"Diaz!" came from Johnny. "He has a hand in everything down here!"

"By the way," he said a moment later, "I have a queer sort of message from my pal here in my pocket. It's all done in figures and signs. How he could expect me to read it is more than I know. And yet, somehow I feel that it must be important."

"Perhaps I can help you. Let me see it."

Johnny drew the crumpled bit of paper from

his pocket, smoothed it out on his knee, then gave it to the girl.

By the light of a tiny flashlight, which Johnny always carried, she studied it for a full three minutes.

" That **is** queer," she said at last, twisting her brow into a puzzled frown. " But somehow it seems easy enough if only one knew how to begin."

For three minutes longer, as the wind sang across the top of their grotto and the rain came dashing down, she studied that bit of paper. Then of a sudden she asked:

" Johnny, how does your friend end his notes to you? "

" Why," said Johnny thoughtfully, " he hasn't written me many. Near as I can recall, when he comes to the end he just stops."

The girl's laugh rang out high and clear.

" I mean does he say, ' Yours truly,' ' Your pal,' or something like that? "

" No." Johnny's answer was prompt. " He always says ' Good luck—Pant.' "

"That's it!" The girl gave a sudden excited jump that brought a shower of small rocks down from above. "That's it! See! Now we are making progress. See! This hyphen stands for g. Those two nines for double o, percentage sign for d, and so on. I know now. This was written on a typewriter, one of the little portable kind."

"Oh!" said Johnny, beginning to see the light. "What a chump I am. Can you make it out?"

"I think I can," she cried excitedly.

"Read it," said Johnny.

"I can't just yet. Let me think. Your typewriter is one of those small portable affairs that fold over and fit into a black case, isn't it?"

"Yes."

"Let me think. I learned the touch system on one of those. Let me feel it out. Got a pencil?"

Johnny produced a stub of what had once been a pencil.

Turning the note over, the girl began drumming on it with all her fingers.

" As if she were playing a piano," thought Johnny.

" There! " She put down a figure. " And there! " she set down a sign.

So at last she filled the back of the sheet with figures and signs.

" Now we can do it," she said at last. " It's all quite simple."

" It would seem so," said Johnny skeptically.

" It really is, only you must know the position of numbers, letters and signs on your typewriter keyboard. If you had studied it out before your typewriter it would have been simple in the extreme.

"Your typewriter has three shifts; one for letters, one for capitals and one for figures and signs. The thing Pant did was to lock his machine for figures and signs, then write his note as if the machine were set for letters. Now I have worked out the location of letters, figures and signs by memory and the touch system, it will be very simple. The figure 5 stands for t, the percent sign for d, and so on."

For a little time longer she studied. Then on a second scrap of paper she wrote the following, which was Pant's note to Johnny, written many days previous:

Johnny:

The map is gone. The Spaniards have it. I am going into the jungle after it. I will get it, never fear. Look out for a Spaniard named Diaz. He is a Devil. Never trust nor believe him for a moment.

Good Luck,

Pant.

"So that was it," Johnny said thoughtfully. "They stole his chart. I only hope he got it back."

Then after a time, "Well, I wish you had seen that note sooner. I did trust Diaz. I did believe him. That was a great mistake."

Still the wind howled and the rain came beating down upon a plantation where thousands of banana stalks lay on the ground.

CHAPTER XIII

A THOUSAND PEARLS

Pant's knees trembled a little as his feet splashed in that bubbling stream that coursed its way through the dreadful Maya cave. It had been strange, the entering of this supposedly haunted cave, with companions. How much more awe inspiring to be entering it alone!

He wondered about those companions of that other adventure. Who was this son of a rich man? What had brought him into the jungle? Where was he now?

As these and many other questions crowded his mind, he made his way cautiously through the outer passages to find himself standing once more on the shore of that curious inland lake which had filled their minds with curiosity on that other visit and so inspired them with fear.

166

He found everything as it had been. The placid surface, sending back a glowing reflection of his light, broke into a thousand ripples as he waded knee deep in its icy waters.

" Clear," was his mental comment. " Can see my toes. What a marvelous reservoir for supplying a city's drinking water! What a pity there is no city near!"

He had waded back to the glistening sands of the beach when, of a sudden, he found his being vibrant to a great expectancy.

" What can it be? " he asked himself. Instantly the answer came.

" The canoe! The canoe on the shore," he told himself. Strange how one's nervous system responds to outer things that his mind does not recall.

" But of course," he assured himself as he neared the spot, " the thing won't give me the shock it once did. We know now that it has been there for two hundred years.

" But wha—"

His gaze covered a space far in advance of

him, many yards beyond the spot where the canoe had stood.

" Gone ! " he muttered, stopping dead in his tracks. " The canoe is gone ! "

Who can say which shock was the greater, the first sudden discovery of the canoe that other time, resting on the beach of this underground lake, or the present astonishing revelation that had come to him?

For a moment he experienced great difficulty in restraining his feet. They appeared ready to carry him back to the entrance. Something within him, an echo of the ancient superstition of his ancestors perhaps, seemed to be insisting that after all this cave was haunted by the spirits of beings who perished long ago and it was they who had ridden away in the mysterious canoe.

For a moment he wavered. Then reason triumphed. " It was Kirk," he told himself. "He has returned with his giant Carib, and for some reason or another has rowed the canoe to some other part of the lake.

"Only question is, would the thing float after all these years?

"Perhaps," he thought, "they did not row it away. That giant of his may have put it on his back and carried it outside. What a treasure for some museum of antiquity!"

The thought that some one had been in the cave since he left it was disturbing. Could it be that Kirk and his Carib, or whoever it may have been, had made a thorough search of the place and had carried away the box of beaten silver.

His heart sank at the thought and he hurried on, reproaching himself for having waited so long before returning.

Yet he had been needed every moment at the chicle camp. It was a great season. The trees were prime, the rainfall abundant. He and his grandfather, with the faithful Caribs, had been working day and night. One long, low, palm-thatched shed was already piled high with bricks of chicle.

"By and by the season will end, then we

will have won," he told himself not realizing that the chicleros' battle is never won until his bricks of chicle are aboard a steamer bound for the United States. Then, and not till then, are his worries at an end.

Pant had dared snatch a day for this adventure. And here he was. Hope vied with fear for a place in his heart as he hurried over the sand toward the entrance to the treasure chamber that might yield a great fortune or offer blank and broken walls to his eager searching gaze.

He climbed the water washed rocks with his heart thumping lustily against his ribs. He entered the small chamber above with the feeling of one who enters some ancient temple at night.

With one quick swing he swept the walls with his keen eyes, then with a low murmured, " Gone! " he sank upon the wet rocks.

Courage and hope conquered disappointment. Rising to his feet, he found himself ready for a more thorough search.

Back behind a tumbled pile of broken bits of rock, thrown in a heap by the earthquake, he caught the dull gleam of some object that was not rock.

With breathless eagerness he attacked the jagged pile. Ten minutes later, with a cry of triumph on his lips, he lifted the beaten silver box from its hiding place.

"Strange!" he murmured. "Still locked. Scarcely a dent in it."

Holding it before him, he shook it vigorously. A rattling sound was the response. His heart raced wildly.

Mopping the perspiration from his brow, he began studying the fastenings that held the cover to its place. There were seven of these. Six were mere clasps that lifted in response to a pry of his clasp knife blade. The seventh, a true lock, resisted vigorously. A sharp blow from the small axe that hung from his belt, severed this and the lid flew up, to reveal such a glistening nest of pink, blue and white pearls as is given to few eyes to see.

"Pearls!" he murmured, scarcely daring to believe his eyes. "A thousand pearls. A king's ransom!"

Then chancing to remember a story he had read as a small boy, he said, "I wonder if they will turn to rough stones and worthless leaves when I reach the sunlight."

This thought troubled him little. The pearls were real enough. Once the six clasps were back in their places, he felt sure enough of being able to bring the box and its contents to the light of day.

"But when I have done this," he thought to himself, "to whom will they belong? To me?"

This problem he considered long and earnestly. The land on which he had found this treasure was wild and rough. No one laid claim to it. But there was the story of the first Don and his beaten silver box of pearls. Was this the box? Were these the pearls? Did they belong by direct inheritance to that last of the Dons who lived now at the foot of the mountain?

" Seems probable," he told himself. " But after all," he concluded, " the real question now is not their ownership, but how are they to be brought safely from this heart of a jungle to the centers of civilization where a thousand pearls may be offered for sale in safety and with a reasonable hope that one may find a buyer. The old Don could never do this. It must be my task."

Having come to this conclusion, he bound the box in a stout brown canvas bag he had brought for the purpose, then began retracing his steps over the way that led to the outer air and sunshine.

Hugging the treasure, he made his way into the chamber of the underground lake. Many and strange were the sensations that passed over him. At times he seemed to hear the cry of terror that escaped the giant Carib's lips as his mind became possessed with fear for the earth god of the Mayas. Unconsciously he found himself looking back, as if expecting to be followed and overtaken by some unseen force that would wrest the treasure from him. Such was the spell of the Maya cave.

At times he fancied that the earth beneath his feet was beginning to tremble and shudder as once it had. He redoubled his speed. But in the end, he knew that this was pure fancy. The water that glimmered at his side was as still as a forest pool at midnight.

He fell to wondering about the canoe that had stood so long by the water's brink. " Who can have been here? Who could have taken it? " he asked himself.

As he asked himself this question, his foot struck some object that, in the silence of the cave, gave off a dry and hollow sound. Leaping back, he threw his flashlight upon the spot.

" A paddle," he murmured, " from the ancient boat."

" Strange they didn't take that with them," he thought after a moment spent in examining it. " Oh well, since they did not, I will. It is elaborately carved and mounted with metal. Looks like gold. A splendid keepsake."

Having picked up the paddle, he threw the light of his torch about him in every direction. Off to the right, further up from the beach, some other object cast dark shadows on the sand. An exclamation escaped his lips as he came close to it.

" A broken bit of a canoe! " he whispered.

Then like a flash it all came to him. " No one has been here," he told himself. " The canoe has not 'been carried away. It was wrecked by the great wave caused by the earthquake."

For a moment he stood gazing upon the bit of ancient wreckage. Then, suddenly realizing that it was growing late, that it was already dark outside the cave, he hurried on.

Darkness had indeed fallen when he reached the outer world of the jungle. This did not trouble him much. He had flashlights and a lantern. There was a trail leading directly to their camp. He would be there in two hours.

" And then," he thought, " what am I to

do with this box of pearls? There are men enough in this wild land who would split my head open for much less than this. They must not know."

As he made his way through the underbrush, now listening to the distant bark of a crocodile and now catching the puh-puh-puh of a jaguar, he pondered the problem of concealing the treasure and of bringing it safely to the outside world.

At last he hit upon what seemed a brilliant idea. The box was the shape of a brick of chicle, only smaller. When he got to camp he would stuff the box with dried palm leaves so it would not rattle, then he would wrap it round and round with other palm leaves.

Having done this, he would remove one of the two bricks of chicle in a gunnysack beneath the storing shed and put in its place the beaten silver box.

"I will mark that sack with a bit of green thread woven in and out of the rough fibre. It will be safe enough until I can decide what to do with it. Does it belong to me, or to the old Don? Guess I better talk it over with my grandfather. He will know what is right."

When he arrived at camp he found everyone asleep but one Carib watchman. As soon as he made himself known to the watchman, he inquired for his grandfather only to learn that at present his grandfather was away, but was expected back in the morning.

When, an hour later, he lay down to rest, the beaten silver box with its priceless contents lay in a coarse gunnysack beside a brick of chicle worth fifty cents a pound. And about it, above, below, on every side were other sacks of chicle.

"I must not let it get out of my sight," he told himself. "I must—" At that he fell asleep.

The journey of the day had been long, his curious experience exhausting. He slept well; too well. When he awoke, the sunlight sifting down through the palm leaves shone upon his face.

His first waking thought was of the beaten silver box. Hurrying into his clothes, he fairly raced to the storing shed. There his eyes fell upon that which left him standing motionless, speechless, struck dumb, paralyzed with fear.

"Gone!" he whispered feebly at last. "The whole pile of chicle at that end is gone, and the silver box with it!"

"The chicle is gone!" he exclaimed to his grandfather a moment later when that old gentleman came into the shed.

"Yes," his grandfather smiled. "Monago and his band of Caribs came in with me at dawn from the north corner of the tract for some supplies. I sent them with four pit-pan loads of chicle down the river. They will bring up supplies. The chicle will be shipped at once. I received word yesterday that the chicle supply was short and that ours should be rushed through to meet the demand."

"Gone!" the boy whispered as he crept away for a few moments of quiet thought.

CHAPTER XIV

HOPE SPRINGS ETERNAL

The end of the storm that had trapped Johnny and Madge Kennedy in the heart of a great banana plantation came suddenly. Clouds went racing. The wind fell. The moon shone again in all its golden glory. It looked down upon a scene of unmatched destruction.

Creeping from their place of refuge which had all but become a pool, they allowed their eyes to sweep the devastated fields.

" It's the end; no doubt of it," said Johnny.

" Looks like the end of the world." There was quiet humor in the girl's tone.

Strange and weird indeed was the scene that confronted them. A palm, its tough stem wrung and twisted by the storm, stood with its fronds hanging down like a nun in prayer.

179

The broken trunks of massive dead trees reared themselves toward the sky. Everywhere the banana plants, which but a few hours before had stood so proudly aloft, now lay flat.

"A hundred thousand bunches," the boy murmured. "And now all gone. What a loss!"

"All gone. I wonder," he murmured as he lifted the topmost plant from off a heap of its fellows. The bunch he cut away with his machete was ready for shipment, and perfect.

"Not a bruise," he said aloud. "Not a banana missing. The plants beneath it formed a pad to ease it down. There must be others, hundreds, thousands, perhaps twenty thousand."

"Here we have bananas!" he exclaimed, turning to Madge Kennedy.

"But they are not ours."

"May as well be. We should be able to buy them. The Fruit Company's boat will not dock for ten days or two weeks. By that time they will be worthless. Come **on, let's** hurry back to the port."

" Diaz won't let you take them."

" That's right," he admitted in sudden **de**spondency. " Of course he won't."

" And yet, I wonder if he'd dare refuse? **"** he said to himself. " He would not be serving the best interests of his master if he did not sell them to us at a salvage price."

He thought of the wary Spaniard's visit **to** Kennedy's home, and of his offer to buy the grapefruit orchard; thought too of the prosperous-looking American he had seen at the foot of the Porte Zelaya dock.

" Wonder if I will ever see that short, stout 'American again? " he thought. " They say he left yesterday morning."

The answer to this last question, though **he** could not know it yet, was a decided yes. He was to meet that mysterious American again under very unusual circumstances. A strange break of fate had predestined them to be thrown together for many days.

As he followed the unerring guidance of the Carib Indian through the maze of fallen trees and destroyed banana plants back toward the port, his thoughts were gloomy indeed. The glory of the tropical moonlight seemed to mock him. Every black mass of twisted banana plants seemed a funeral pile on which his dead hopes were to be burned.

"Fate treats one strangely at times," he told himself.

So it seemed. He had been endeavoring to assist a very worthy, aged and needy man, one who had given all his life to others. This man had fought for his country, fearlessly at the front of his command, yet he refused the honor of being called "Captain."

The World War was not the only one in which he had fought. Time and again the need of his humble fellow countrymen, the black Caribs whose fathers and mothers had been Indians and negro slaves, had called him to his duty, and he had gone.

On one occasion, during the terrible yellow-fever plague, he had toiled days without end, burying the Carib dead and caring for the stricken ones until the hand of the dread enemy was stayed.

"Not a native in all Stann Creek district but knows and loves him," Johnny told himself. "And now, in his old age, when he truly needs a lift and we try to help him, see how things come out! We are blocked by a scheming Spaniard who never fought for any country, nor for the good of any person beside himself. He probably never had an unselfish thought in the whole of his life."

His thoughts were gloomy enough. But, after climbing over many obstructions and wading numerous small, swollen streams, he began to reason with himself. What was this "Fate" he was always thinking of? Was it the great Creator, or was it some other being?

As he looked away at the golden moon, a line of poetry came to him.

"God's in His Heaven,
All's right with the world."

"I wonder?" he thought. Then, "How absurd! Of course it's true. Somehow there must still be a way."

His first visible justification of this faith came to him the moment he stepped inside the dock office. There, snugly sleeping on a couch in the corner, was a slender, dark-skinned child whose black eyelashes were long and lovely. And there, pacing the floor before her, was her father, the great plantation owner.

"Don del Valle!" the boy exclaimed. He could scarcely believe his eyes.

"Yes, Senor Johnny Thompson." The man's tone seemed austere.

"I—I am truly sorry that your crop has been ruined," said the boy.

"And I, sir, am disappointed in you, disappointed that you should have taken advantage of my endeavor to deal generously with you."

"How—how—I—" the boy stammered.

"Excuses are unnecessary. You told me you had a ship. Where is that ship? You said

you would take twenty thousand bunches.
Where are they? Are they on the ship? They
are there." He waved his hand toward the
devastated plantation.

Johnny's head whirled. What was this—
more treachery?

"Our boat," he said in as quiet a tone as
he could command, "was at your dock three
days. In such a storm you could not expect
her to hold to her moorings. Where is she
now? Who knows? Perhaps at the bottom
of the sea. The reason she left without a
cargo was that your manager, Senor Diaz,
would not supply it."

"Is this true?" The dark eyes of the
Honduran capitalist bored him through and
through.

"Ask any workman on the dock or in the
village. If he has not been corrupted by a
scoundrel, he will tell you it is true."

Whirling about, the man shot a few sharp
questioning words in Spanish to a boy who
sat half asleep in the corner.

Starting up, the boy answered rapidly.

"He says," Don del Valle turned slowly about, "that all you have told me is the truth. It is my honor to beg your most humble pardon. You have been badly treated. Ask me some favor and I will grant it."

Johnny's heart beat fast. His mind worked like some speeding mechanism.

"Shall I?" he asked himself. "I will."

"In the name of one who deserves much, our friend Donald Kennedy, I shall ask one favor."

"Ask it."

"That you sell me the crop of bananas on this plantation."

"They are worthless. The storm has ruined them."

"Not all. There is still a ship load of good ones."

"How can I grant such a request? I am under contract to deliver these bananas to the Fruit Company."

"No contract," Johnny's voice vibrated

with earnestness, "stands before an act of God. The storm was an act of God. No Fruit Company's ship will be here within ten days. By that time it will be too late."

"You are right. Your request is granted. To-morrow I will send my men into the field."

"By your leave," said Johnny quickly, "I will buy them as they are in the field. I will gather and load them myself."

The owner gave him a piercing look, then having recalled Johnny's past experience, he said slowly:

"Very well. This also is granted. You may use my equipment. Ten cents a bunch in the field, a salvage price."

There was a slight move at the door. To-gether they turned to look. There stood Diaz. His white face showed that he had heard much, understood all.

Don del Valle pointed a finger of accusation and scorn at him.

He vanished into the dark. His plotting was not at an end, however. He went directly to a long shed where many men, beachcombers, longshoremen, chicleros and banana gatherers, were sleeping. There he began to sow the seeds of a hasty revolution and a wild demonstration against the hated white men, which was destined once more to threaten disaster to Johnny Thompson's plans.

Early that morning one might have found Johnny alone at the edge of the banana plantation. To one unaccustomed to Johnny's ways, his actions might have seemed strange. Was he taking his daily dozen? Perhaps, but surely they were a queer dozen.

If you know Johnny at all you are aware of the fact that he is a skillful boxer. But down there in the tropics bare hands avail little. Johnny was not shadow boxing. The thing he was doing was quite different. He was keeping fit all the same.

A stout young mahogany tree had sprung up in the midst of the banana field. From a tough limb of this tree Johnny had suspended a large bunch of bananas. The top of the bunch was a little higher than Johnny's shoulders, the tip a foot from the ground.

Seizing one of two machetes, great long bladed knives like swords, that lay on the ground, the boy began circling the swinging bunch of bananas as one might a mortal enemy. Brandishing his machete, he circled this imaginary enemy three times. Then, as if an opening had appeared, he made a sudden onslaught that sent green bananas thudding to earth and set the bunch spinning wildly.

Then he parried and thrust as an imaginary blade sang close to his head. Once more, with a lightning-like swing, he sprang in. This time he split a single banana from end to end and sent the severed halves soaring high.

He sprang back. No true blade could have inspired greater skill than the boy displayed before an empty world and without a real adversary.

The battle ended when with one swift stroke he severed the stem in the middle and with a sweeping twirl sent it thudding down.

" Cut his head off!" he chuckled, throwing himself upon the ground to mop the perspiration from his brow.

" It's like boxing," he thought, " this great Central American sport of machete fighting, only—it's different. You feel as if only half of you were in it."

As a boxer Johnny was neither right nor left handed. He was ambidextrous. Therein lay much of his power. How few of us ever learn to use both hands well. Yet what an advantage comes to those who do.

" That's the trouble with this machete business," he now thought to himself. " Only one hand, that's all you use. And yet, why not?"

He sprang to his feet, selected a second bunch of bananas, hung it on high, then prepared as before to attack it. This time, however, he wielded a machete in each hand.

At first he found it awkward. Once he barely missed cutting his own wrist. By the time he had demolished three other bunches he felt that he was making progress and that an ambidextrous fighter with two knives would have a decided advantage over one who fought with a single blade.

Johnny, as you may have guessed, was preparing for that moment which he felt must come sooner or later, when he and Diaz would stand face to face ready to fight their battle out with the great Central American blade.

"And when that time comes," he told himself, " it must not find me unprepared."

CHAPTER XV

UNSEEN FOES

It was night, such a night as only the tropics knows. Night, dead calm, hot, and no moon. Motionless clouds hanging low, and dark. Such a darkness as Pant had never before known hung over all.

Ten feet below him was the sea. He sensed rather than saw it, felt the long rolling lift of its swells as the Carib sailing boat gently rose and fell.

They were a mile out to sea, becalmed. There should be no one near them. There had been no craft near when darkness fell. In such a calm no boat could sail, and who would care to row on such a hot, oppressive night? Yet, strange as it may seem, from time to time he imagined that some faint sound came drifting in from the black void that engulfed them.

" It can't be," he told himself. " There was no one near at sunset. There is no one now. That silver box of pearls has gotten on my nerves. I will go to sleep and forget it all."

He did not sleep at once. His mind was filled with many things. His pursuit of the pit-pan loads of chicle which his grandfather had sent down the river had been a strenuous one. A pit-pan, the seventy foot dugout of the Carib country, when manned by a score of expert boatmen, is a swift river craft. Without giving his grandfather any definite reason for his sudden departure, he had hired a twelve foot dugout from a native bushman and had set out in pursuit of the chicle sack that contained his treasure of pearls in a beaten silver box. For long hours, eating little, scarcely sleeping at all, he had held on in pursuit. At the end of the second day his frail craft had shot boldly out into the ocean. There he met the pit-pans on their return trip.

For the moment he counted all lost. When they told him that the chicle had been stowed away aboard a Carib sailing vessel manned by his grandfather's men and bound for Belize, his spirits rose.   An hour later found him aboard that boat, munching dry casaba bread and talking to the Caribs between bites.

He had not told them why he had come, but gave them to understand that he was to sail to Belize with them.

"In Belize," he told himself, "before the chicle is brought aboard the steamer, I will claim my precious bag. It will be time enough to decide then what the next move shall be.

"And now here we are becalmed," he thought to himself with a low shudder.

Strange and terrible things had happened in these waters.   They had been the hunting grounds of buccaneers. As he closed his eyes he seemed to hear the creaking of windlasses, the heavy breathing of men in the dark, the boom of cannon, the rattle of muskets, the ring thud of steel.

"Those days are gone," he told himself, shaking himself free from the illusion.   But were they? Only the year before four black men, who had engaged to carry two rich traders across the bay, had murdered their passengers and sailed to some unknown haven with their spoils.

"Always a little danger down here," he thought. "Revolutions and all that."

He rose suddenly on an elbow, to listen intently. Sure as he was a rational human being, out of that darkness had come a sound.

With a hand that trembled slightly, he touched a dark form close beside him. Something there stirred; otherwise there was not a sound.

"Hist!" His whisper was low and tense. "Not a word! There is some one."

"Who? Where?" came back still in a whisper.

"Who knows, Tuan? You listen. Your ears are better than mine."

"Tish!" came the black-brown man's low expression of appreciation, then all was silence once more.

Tuan was one of those Caribs who, somewhere back in the dim distance, had a black
slave for an ancestor. A great gaunt man,
he was endowed with the strength of the
black race and the endurance of the red man.
A lifetime in the bush had given him the ear
of a jaguar.

"Tish!" he whispered a moment later.
"Truly there came a sound. But who can it
be? Our other schooner is near. They may
have put off a dory."

"But why?"

"There is no reason."

Silence once more. A swell larger than
those that went before lifted the boat high,
tilted her to a rakish angle, then let her fall.
The boom rattled, the lazy sail flapped. After
that the silence was greater than before.

To Pant the situation was a trying one. He
found himself only a passenger on a boat
chartered by his grandfather. He had no
authority here. If he had, would he awaken
the crew? He hardly knew. One does not

suspect a single sound. In the tropics not all who come near are rascals.

And yet, aboard that schooner, or its mate lying close alongside, was the gunnysack with the green thread running through it—a rude container for a rich treasure.

"If I should lose it now!" His breath came short at the thought. He had risked his life for a treasure which he somehow felt did not belong to him, but which, nevertheless, he was now morally bound to preserve.

Suddenly his thoughts broke short off.

"There! There!" he whispered hoarsely.

But Tuan was on his feet. He was striking out at something in the dark. His eyesight was quite as remarkable as his hearing.

There came a loud splash. Tuan had not gone overboard, but some one had.

"We are being boarded," was the thought that shot through the boy's mind as he struggled to his feet.

But what was this? There came a second splash, another, and yet another.

"The chicle!" he exclaimed out loud, unthinking. "They are throwing it overboard!" The deck was piled high with gunnysacks filled with chicle. Was the sack of the green thread among them? He had come aboard too late to know. Were these boarding ruffians Diaz's men, or were they of another sort? Had they somehow learned of the treasure? Were they after that?

"How could they know?" he asked himself.

His head whirled. What was to be done? He took a step forward and instantly collided with some bulky object.

At once he found himself grappling with the oily body of a native. Over and over they rolled on the deck. They bumped first into a heap of chicle, then into the gunwale. This last appeared to stun his opponent. Seizing the opportunity, he grasped him by an arm and leg to send him overboard.

He caught the call of Tuan, heard the Caribs swarming up from below, listened for a second to blows that fell all about him; then, finding himself within a circle of sudden light, staggered backward to fall clumsily, and to at last pitch backward into the sea.

He struck out in the direction he hoped was right for the ship. The sea was warm as dish water. Sharks and crocodiles lurked everywhere. He must get aboard.

"And then what?" he asked himself.

About him sounded cries, calls, blows, signs of wild confusion. Then came the creak of oarlocks.

"A dory! Our dory from the other boat. Reinforcements!" Hope arose.

His hand touched something hard.

"A bag of chicle," he thought. "Supposing it was the bag of the green thread."

The thing was buoyant. Dragging himself upon it, he took time to look about him. A light flared here, then went out. A torch flamed, shot upward, circled down, hissed in the water and went out. The circle of a flashlight revealed four men in deadly embrace.

"Got to get back. They need me." Having found the direction of the boat, he swam quickly to it. There, having made his way cautiously about it, and coming into contact with a dugout that most certainly was not their own, he capsized and sunk it.

A little further on his hand gripped a rope. A moment later he was aboard the schooner again.

Suddenly a bright light streamed out. Some one had lighted a gas lantern and hung it high on the mast.

"That will end it," he thought.

It did, for him. An iron belaying pin, hurled square at him, took him in the temple. After that, for several hours, he knew no more.

CHAPTER XVI

IN BATTLE ARRAY

At dawn of the day after the hurricane, Don del Valle and his beautiful black-eyed daughter hastened away in his high powered motor boat. That he might determine the amount of damage done by the storm, it was necessary for him to leave for his other plantation at once. Johnny Thompson went to the wireless station to begin a search in air for the *North Star* and her courageous captain.

" If she has been wrecked, or if she has been carried far by storm, and the skipper refuses to return, we are lost," he said to Madge Kennedy.

For an hour he sent out messages. Each moment he became more depressed. What if the ship had been lost?

" One more evil happening to be charged

against my too impetuous desire to be of service," he groaned.

"Let us hope it has not happened," said
the girl. "Captain Jorgensen has sailed these
seas for many years. He is hardly the man
to lose his vessel."

"Good news!" Johnny exclaimed a moment
later when he was brought a message. "The
North Star is anchored behind Mutineer's
Island, all safe and sound. I will get off a
message instructing them to pull away for
our own dock at once. There we will pick
up your crates of grapefruit and a hundred or
so of your Caribs. We will bring them here
to gather and load the bananas. They can
be trusted. I put no faith in the half-castes
that swarm about this dock. We have been
defeated by them once. Once is enough for
me.

"Oh, I tell you!" he exclaimed, seizing the
girl by the hand and doing a wild Indian dance
across the floor, "we'll win yet!"

"You forget," said the girl soberly, "that

the great, all-powerful organization, the Fruit Company, may block your sales after you arrive in New York."

But Johnny could not be disheartened. The ship was his. The bananas were his also. He had men to gather and load them. New York and the day of their arrival were far away.

" 'Sufficient unto the day is the evil thereof,' " he quoted, then hurried to get off a message to Kennedy. With Kennedy on the job, the grapefruit would be ready to load, and the Caribs prepared to steam away with them to the dock here at Porte Zelaya.

Johnny was soon enough to know that this day's evil was indeed sufficient unto itself. He had not left the wireless room before bad news arrived. The giant Carib, who had come in a motor boat to Porte Zelaya, and who had been with Johnny and Madge in the storm, had been loafing about the dock with his ears open. Those ears had caught snatches of terrible things. He told Madge of all this in his native tongue.

"What is it?" Johnny asked as he saw the look of terror creep into her eys.

"A plot!" She said the words through white, set lips. "That rascal Diaz, who was discharged from his position as foreman, is plotting to destroy your plans, and you with them."

"How? How could he?"

"He is stirring up a revolution. He is telling the ignorant half-castes that the white men rule their country, that they have been paid very little for much hard work, and that now they are to be deprived of that work altogether, that you are to bring a ship load of Caribs from Stann Creek to do the work which is rightfully their own."

"That in part is true," said Johnny. "I wonder if, after all, I am wrong? Would they do the work if I were to offer it?"

Madge consulted the Carib. He shook his head and waved his hands in wild gestures.

"He says they would not work," interpreted the girl, "that their blood is hot, that they lust for battle and that they will meet us at the dock with clubs and machetes—a hundred, two hundred, perhaps three hundred strong. They want a fight."

" Very well." Johnny's tone was deep and strong. " They shall have a fight, if fight there must be. We are within our rights."

He stepped back to the wireless to send one more message. The message which went to Kennedy, ran;

" Have every able-bodied Carib at Stann Creek at the dock, every man armed."

Ten minutes later their motor boat was popping, and the dock and low sheds of Porte Zelaya were fading in the distance.

When Johnny and Madge, riding on the prow of the motor boat with the giant Carib at the wheel, rounded a point of land and came in sight of the dock at Stann Creek, they were given the thrill of their young lives. The dock was one moving mass of men.

" The Caribs ! " A lump came to the girl's throat.

" They came," said Johnny.

" I knew they would. They would do anything for grandfather."

It was true. The instant Johnny's word from the air had arrived, messengers had been sent helter-skelter, here, there, everywhere. The train on the narrow gauge railroad had gone into the bush to return groaning and creaking with such a load of black and brown humanity as had never before been seen on the backwaters of Central America.

Every grown Carib within twenty miles of the dock was there. The instant the *North Star* came alongside they swarmed upon the deck.

The loading of the grapefruit with the aid of so many strong and willing hands was but the work of a few hours. Then, with a load of humanity greater than her load of fruit, the ship cast off her moorings and headed straight for the dock at Porte Zelaya where, Johnny felt sure, there awaited them a great and terrible battle.

As the boy walked the deck his eyes shone with joy. Whoever commanded a stronger, braver, more loyal army than the black throng that, swarming up the hatches, perched themselves on mast and rigging, forecastle, after deck and anchor, until there was scarcely space left to move?

As his eyes swept the deck they lighted with a sudden new joy. They had fallen upon a figure garbed in a dress of gorgeous golden yellow. The one white girl of the company, the queen of all the Stann Creek region, had not deserted them. There, on a coil of rope beside her patriarchal grandfather, sat Madge Kennedy, smiling her very best.

"It's great! Great!" Johnny murmured. "And yet—"

His brow clouded. There was to be a fight. The thing seemed inevitable. It would be a bloody battle. He knew well enough what these battles between Caribs and half-castes meant. Once, on the far reaches of the Rio Hondo, he had witnessed such a battle. It had been a rather terrible affair. As he closed his eyes now he heard the thwack of mahogany clubs on unprotected heads, caught the swish of great swinging knives, saw the agony of hatred and fear on dark faces where blood ran free.

"I said then I hoped I'd never see another such battle," he told himself, "and yet here we are driving straight on toward one that promises to be quite as terrible."

Before him, sitting astride the rail, was a Carib youth. "Can't be over eighteen," Johnny mused.

He had never in his life seen a more cheerful, smiling face. To look at him, to catch the glint of his eye, the gleam of his white teeth, to see the rollicking movement of his face, was like viewing a wonderful waterfall against a glorious sunset.

Could it be that before this day was done that glorious face might be still in death?

For a moment Johnny felt like turning back. What was success, even success in a righteous cause, when it must be purchased at such a cost?

"And yet," he reasoned, "we cannot turn back. The right must be defended. It must always be so. Perhaps there is a way to avert it, but come what may, we must go on."

Having arrived at this conclusion, he walked quietly down the deck to take his place beside Donald Kennedy and his granddaughter.

For some time they talked in low tones, the man and the boy, and the girl listened. Little wonder that they talked earnestly. Much was at stake.

"It might work," said Johnny at last. "Anyway, we'll try it. You can talk to them in Spanish."

That was the end of conversation. After that they sat there looking and listening. From somewhere forward there came the rattle of a banjo, the tom-tom-tom of a snake-head drum. Aft, the chant of a weird song rose and fell with the boat.

" They don't realize they are going to war," said Johnny.

" That's the pity. They never do," said the girl, shading her eyes to gaze away at the perfect blue of the lovely Caribbean Sea.

All too soon the thrum of the banjo ceased, the tom-tom of the drum became muffled and low. Land, the point of Porte Zelaya, had been sighted.

Rising, the girl and the old man made their way along the deck. As they moved along they spoke in low tones to the men and the men, as if moved by some magic spell, rose slowly to go shuffling forward or aft, and to disappear down the hatchways, leaving the decks almost deserted.

When the *North Star* came within hailing distance of the dock, which was swarming with half-castes drawn up in battle array, a little group of some fifty black Caribs were gathered on the forward deck of the *North Star*. That was all. Not a pike pole nor machete was in sight. They seemed only a small group of laborers prepared for a day's work of gathering and loading bananas.

A breathless expectancy hung over all the ship as it came in close, reversed her engines, dropped anchor and stood off the wharf for further orders.

The great man of the jungle, Donald Kennedy, tall, stately of bearing, yet humble, stepped forward to the rail and began to speak in quiet tones to the throng on the deck.

At once there arose a terrific shout.

" Down with the white man! Death to the intruder!"

These words were shouted in Spanish, but Johnny knew their meaning well enough. He thrilled and shuddered. Pike poles were tossed in air above the dock, great knives flashed in the sun, a pistol exploded. What was to be the end of it all?

Again came comparative silence. Again the aged man spoke. Patiently, as if speaking to children, he began.

Again he was interrupted by cries of;

"Death! Destruction! Down with the white man!"

Four times, with steady patience, the great man attempted to make himself heard.

At last, realizing the futility of it all, he turned and shouted three words in the Carib tongue.

Instantly there came from the black men forward a shout to answer that of the half-castes on the dock. At the same time, pike-poles and machetes flashed and four streams of humanity, black and menacing, began pouring up the hatchways.

Johnny Thompson thrilled and grew deathly cold at sight of them. They swarmed up the masts, they filled the deck, they straddled the rail and crowded the roofs of the cabins. Everywhere weapons gleamed. From every corner rang the defiant shout of Caribs ready to defend with their lives the rights of Kennedy, whom they had come to think of as a loyal friend.

No pirate ship that sailed these waters in

days that are gone ever witnessed a more tremendous and startling demonstration.

Before it, awed into silence, the mob on the dock fell back, then began slipping away. One by one they slunk off into the bush. In ten minutes time not a man was left. A bloodless victory had been won. The field was theirs.

CHAPTER XVII

PANT'S PROBLEM INCREASES

When Pant awoke from many bad dreams, he found himself in a cool and comfortable bed on shore. A doctor was bending over him.

" That's fine, old boy," the doctor was saying. " Now you'll do. You got quite a welt on the head. But your jolly old bean is hard. Never cracked it a mite."

" But the treasure box!" Pant exclaimed, still unable to think clearly, or use caution. " Where is it? "

" The treasure box? I see you are still a little off in the head. Here, take this; it will clear you up," said the doctor.

Pant took the contents of the glass held out to him at a single draught and without a question. In the meantime his head cleared. He said no more about the box of pearls, but learned by judicious questioning that the attacking band had on the night before been driven off with little loss of men or goods. A few sacks of chicle had drifted away in the night, that was all.

"And if one of them has a green thread running through the sack!" he thought to himself, and was thrown into a near panic.

"And the schooners?" he asked suddenly. "Where are they?"

"Got a fair wind and sailed this morning for Belize. Must be there by now."

"They'll load the chicle aboard the Torentia?"

"Naturally."

"And she sails—"

"In about twenty-four hours."

"Doctor!" exclaimed the boy sitting straight up in bed and gripping his arm hard. "Fix me up someway. I've got to get over to Belize. At once! Right away, doctor. This very minute!"

"Well, young fellow," said the doctor,

rescuing his arm and putting on a wry face as he rubbed it vigorously, " you seem to have plenty of strength. I'll see what I can do."

A half hour later, a trifle unsteady on his feet, but otherwise quite himself, Pant was making his way to the water front of Stann Creek, the port to which he was carried after the battle. He felt the heavy bandages about his head, blinked at the sunlight, looked this way then that, until spying what appeared to be a small store just before him, he hurried in.

" I want a boat," he said to the black proprietor.

" What kind of a boat? "

" Any boat that will take me to Belize."

" No boat go to-day." The man settled back in his corner.

" You mean they won't go to-day? " The boy's brow wrinkled.

" No go."

" Not for any price? "

" Oh! Special trip, go. Maybe. You got twenty dollars? "

Pant hesitated. He had twenty dollars and a little change. To part with it all would seem to be courting disaster. But much was at stake. He threw all in the balance.

" Yes, I have twenty dollars. Where is the boat? "

" Me see." The man held out a hand. Pant showed him two golden eagles.

" My boat sailing boat. Good boat. Very fast boat. Ready to go, fifteen minutes." At sight of the gold the man went into action.

Action on land is one thing. On sea it is quite another. They were half way up the bay when the wind fell. The sail fell with it, and the boat stood still in a placid sea.

For two precious hours the boy with a bruised and aching head lay beneath a pitiless tropical sun. Then the merciful after dinner breeze came up and at once they went booming along.

Nothing can be more delightful than a sail in a Carib boat on the Caribbean Sea. To lie on deck and sense the lifting glide of the prow, to feel the cool breeze on your face, to see the water go rippling by, that is joy indeed. Pant would have enjoyed it to the full had not his mind been vexed by many questions. Would he reach Belize in time or would the steamer be gone? Was the chicle sack of the green thread still on the sailing boat of the night before, or had the marauders carried it away? If it were still on board, if it went to America and he did not go with it, what then? Would he recover the treasure?

"Not a chance," he told himself. "I must have been out of my head to hide the box in such a place. But now I must see it through.

"Why must I?" he asked himself, and at once came the answer, "The old Don." Unconsciously he had come to think of the treasure of pearls as belonging as much to the aged Don as to himself. And to that man he owed much. He had, beyond doubt, once saved his grandfather's life.

They were nearing Belize. The white houses with their red roofs showed in the distance. And, joy of joys! There to the left was the *Torentia* riding at anchor.

Still there was much to fear. She might at any moment weigh anchor and put out to sea.

"And after all," he said to himself, "what am I to do? By this time the chicle is stowed away. Dare I make a clean breast of my story? I wouldn't dare trust them. What then? I must go with the ship to New York. But I have no money. Who is to pay my passage?" Surely here was a situation.

"I will find a way. I must!"

And in the end he did. Sailing time was only a half hour off when he climbed the rope ladder to the deck of the *Torentia*.

"Hello, brother," said the purser, looking at his bandaged head. "What revolution did you come from? Did they make you President or only commander of the navy?"

"Neither," said Pant with a grin that went far. "I want to go to New York."

"Got any money?"

"No."

" Can't go."

" That last shipment of chicle you took on board belonged to my grandfather. I'll wire him for money in New York."

" There's lots of broke Americans down here. They've all got rich relatives."

" I'll prove it." Sitting down upon the hatch, Pant told things about Colonel Longstreet that went far to prove that he at least was a boon companion of the old man.

" Guess you're square," said the purser at last. " Anyway, I'll take a chance. Steward will fix you up later."

By careful inquiry Pant learned that the chicle had been stored beneath the forward hatch. The hatch was kept open. There were twenty thousand bunches of bananas on board. They must have air. By leaning far over the hatch he could see ends of the chicle bags. Was the one he wanted there?

" Can't be sure," he warned himself. " Too dark down there. " Have to get closer," he said. " Will, too, after a while. See if I don't."

CHAPTER XVIII

TWO BLADE JOHNNY

On the dock at Porte Zelaya, the task of loading bananas was at last progressing. At regular intervals all that long forenoon and well into the day, the little engine with its string of cars came puffing and rattling down the narrow gauge track. With its cars groaning under the great loads of green which it brought, it came to a halt on the dock. There, in exact imitation of the ants that had entertained Johnny on the previous day, the barefooted, perspiring Caribs seized upon the precious fruit, to pass it from hand to hand and store it carefully away in the hold of the ship.

Johnny, with an eye out for trouble, was everywhere. Now on the dock, now on the train and now in the heart of the banana plantation, his keen eye took in everything. Yet no trouble came. A few disconsolate Spanish banana workers hung about. Such of these as seemed willing to render honest service Johnny set to work.

Dressed in the simplest of garb, cotton shirt, khaki trousers and high-topped boots, Johnny nevertheless drew forth many a covert smile from the black Caribs, for he wore at his belt not one machete, but two—one on either side, and none of the Caribs had ever before seen a man carry two such weapons.

The sun was hanging low over the storm wrecked banana plantation, their task was well nigh completed when Johnny, seeing some straggling young banana plants growing in a half cleared patch to the right of the track and believing that here he might find a few superb bunches, hurried away down a narrow deer trail.

He had reached the nearest bunch of bananas and was about to cut it down when something sprang at him.

His first thought, as his heart went racing

and he dropped to earth with the quickness of a cat, was that he had come close to the lair of a jaguar.

This thought was dispelled by the white gleam of a blade.

"Diaz!" he told himself. "And we are alone. There is to be a battle after all, a battle, perhaps to the death, with weapons which he has been familiar with since a child."

One thought gave him courage as, springing away to the right, fighting for time to draw a blade, hotly pursued by the panting Spaniard, he rounded a great mahogany tree.

Having drawn his right hand blade, he took a stand in a raised spot offering some slight-advantage.

His crafty opponent did not rush him. Instead he attempted to outmaneuver him by springing first to right, then to left, to at last completely circle him.

"You'll not win by that," thought Johnny as the blood still pounded at his temples. "That is like boxing."

This maneuvering gave him time for a few darting thoughts as to how the affair was to end. If he were killed, what then? He hoped his body might be found at once. Madge Kennedy would never consent to the ship's starting without him, dead or alive. That he knew well enough. He wanted this, his last undertaking, to succeed, wanted it desperately.

"Somehow I must outmaneuver him," he thought. At once his mind turned to that extra blade.

There was no time for drawing it, for of a sudden his opponent, with blade lifted high, sprang squarely at him. Had Johnny been beneath that blade when it fell, his skull must have been split. With skill acquired as a boxer, he leaped away and the machete, slipping from the Spaniard's unnerved hand, dropped harmless on the moss.

There was no time for Johnny to seize his opponent's blade. There was opportunity to draw his left hand blade. Draw it he did.

The expression on the Spaniard's dark and

angry face as he found himself facing two blades was strange to see. Plainly he was puzzled and nonplussed. He had fought and beyond doubt done for more than one man who, like himself, wielded a single machete. But what of this boy who seemed at home with two?

He wasted little time in thought, but springing with a twisting glide, he attempted to throw Johnny off his guard. In this he was not successful.

For a full quarter of an hour, battling, perspiring, crossing blades, bending, thrusting, each striving for an advantageous opening, the two men fought on.

Then a sudden catastrophe threatened. On stepping backward Johnny caught his heel in a tie-tie vine that grew low to the ground. The next instant, with the Spaniard all but on top of him, he went crashing to earth.

With a look that was terrible to see, the Spaniard aimed what he meant to be a final blow.

A hush hung over the jungle. The blade came swinging down. But not too fast. As if dodging a boxer's blow, Johnny shot his head to one side. Burying itself a half blade's length in the ooze, the knife struck there. Nor did it come away when the frantic Spaniard pulled at it. It had become firmly embedded in the buried stump of a mahogany tree.

The next instant the Spaniard felt himself lifted bodily in air. Then with senses reeling he came crashing down.

When he came to himself he found himself bound hand and foot. After crashing him to earth, Johnny had made use of the tie-tie vine which had come near bringing him to his end. With it he had bound his opponent hand and foot.

"You villian! You dirty dog!" Johnny hissed in his ear. "I should kill you. You have no right to live, you who strike when a man is down. But I will spare you. The ants may crawl over you for a few hours. After that I will send some one."

Gathering up three blades, souvenirs of the expedition, he disappeared into the brush.

Ten hours later, laden to capacity with the golden harvest of the tropics, the *North Star* pointed her prow toward the north, while the Caribs, now crowded into pit-pans and sail-boats, headed for home, lifting their voices in song-like chants.

Only one little thing occurred to interrupt the *North Star's* passage out of the Caribbean Sea into the open ocean. The evening was calm. They chanced upon a sailing boat lying becalmed and helpless in the midst of the sea. On the deck of the boat was a prosperous looking man. Short and stout, and with a very red face, he looked the part of a very busy man who thought well of his importance in the world of affairs, and who had by some chance been caught in an eddy from which he could not well extricate himself.

He requested that they take him aboard.

Johnny told him that he was not sure that coming aboard the steamer would serve his purpose. The man insisted; in fact he appeared to act as though he owned the *North Star*. So aboard he came.

"What boat is this?" he demanded.

"The *North Star*," said Johnny quietly.

"When did we charter her?"

"When did who charter her?"

"The Fruit Company, of course." The man's tone was overbearing.

"You didn't." Johnny's tone was still quiet. "I did."

The man sniffed the air. "Bananas!" he said. "I am President of the Fruit Company, and in that capacity I demand to know what is the business of this steamer in these waters."

Johnny's heart suddenly sprang up into his throat. He tried to speak and could not. His head whirled. The President of the great corporation here on board his ship! The very man who had the power to make or break not alone him, but Kennedy and Madge as well. The thing seemed impossible!

" F—fruit," he stammered. " She carries fruit. Bananas, and for—forbidden fruit and —and things like that."

He knew he was talking like an idiot, but for the life of him he could not talk sense. Little wonder. He was having his first little chat with a millionaire, but it was not to be his last.

CHAPTER XIX

THE UNWILLING GUEST

" Do you mean to say," said the magnate who had been taken on board the *North Star,* "that this ship is loaded with bananas from Central America, and that it is not chartered by our Company? "

" Bananas and grapefruit." Johnny was gaining control of himself. What if this were a millionaire? What if it was in his power to make or break them? He couldn't very well do that before they arrived in New York, and that metropolis was a long way off.

" Then, sir," said the capitalist, " you have been trespassing. This is forbidden cargo."

" Who forbids it? "

Without answering the man stared at him for a moment. His next remark was guarded.

" You couldn't get a cargo anywhere along

the coast without bribing some one or taking the cargo by force."

Hot words leaped to Johnny's lips. He was no thief. He had bribed no one. He left them unsaid.

Instead, he watched the sailing boat, from which the man had been taken, fade in the distance.

" We'll let it stand at that," he said quietly. " In the meantime, where were you going? "

" Going from Bacaray to Belize in that worthless sailboat manned by spotted Caribs. My motor boat was wrecked in the storm. The sail boat was becalmed, and there we were. Lay there for ten hours."

" Belize? " Johnny wrinkled his brow. He did not wish to touch at this capitol of British Honduras. The Fruit Conmpany was strong there. Who could tell but that fruit inspectors or health inspectors, in sympathy with the Fruit Company, perhaps bribed by them, would hold his ship off those shores until his bananas were overripe and ruined.

" Having him on board makes it worse," he told himself. Again his brow wrinkled.

A happy thought struck him.

" You are planning to stay in Belize for some time? "

" Going back to New York on our boat the *Arion*. She was to touch at Belize. Took on her load at Puerte Baras."

Johnny heaved a sigh of relief. " The *Arion* sailed six hours ago. It gives me great pleasure to offer you my stateroom and a passage to New York."

Johnny's smile irritated the man. His face turned red. He seemed about to choke.

" You—you'll touch at Belize! " he stormed.

" Belize," said Johnny calmly, " is four hours off our course. We are headed for the open sea, and eventually for New York. I don't like to seem pig-headed, nor over important, but we are not going to alter our course."

In this he was wrong. He was destined to alter his course in a manner that was pleasing to no one.

"You will take me to Belize or I will have you up in the Marine Court."

"You'll not have much of a case," said Johnny. "You were adrift. We picked you up at your own request. The law allows us to charge you for your passage to our own port. We'll pass that up. You may as well make yourself comfortable. We will dock at New York in good time."

"A very cold day when you dock in New York with this—"

The man checked his speech with difficulty, then turning on his heel, went stamping down the deck.

He had said enough. Johnny guessed that he had a scorpion on board.

"When the time comes he'll bite," he told himself.

For a moment he considered turning about and heading for Belize. This thought was dismissed in a moment.

"Won't do it," he told himself shortly. "That would double his chances of defeating us. If he didn't tie us up in Belize, he'd wire New York and his entire pack would be upon us. As it is he can't get off a word before he reaches New York. That gives us a fighting chance."

"Looks as if Providence was kind in sending him to us," he added.

He turned and hurried forward to prepare his stateroom for the Unwilling Guest, and there was a smile on his face.

*   *   *   *   *

"It really isn't necessary to tell all you know." Kennedy said this in a friendly drawl, as he sat beside Johnny on the forward deck. Madge Kennedy was there too. Johnny had persuaded the old man to come along with him on the *North Star.* "The passage," he had argued, " will cost you nothing. Captain Jorgensen is coming back for that cargo of cocoanuts and chicle. He'll be glad to bring you down. You may be able to help me a lot in disposing of the fruit. Anyway, the trip will do you good."

So here they were, three good pals, an old man, a young man and a girl.

Johnny did not reply to Kennedy's remark about not telling all you know.

" I told a man once the location of a mahogany tract I meant to buy," Kennedy went on. " It was good mahogany, some of it six feet through, five thousand feet to the tree. I told that man and he went before me and bought it. I talked too much then. I've learned better."

" That Unwilling Guest of yours," he drawled after a time, " that President of the Fruit Company, has been on board twenty-four hours and has never showed his head out of his stateroom. Even pays the steward to bring his meals to him. That right? "

Johnny nodded.

" Nice, friendly sort of a millionaire. That right? Perhaps he thinks we're not worth talking to."

" Johnny," the old man laid a hand gently on the boy's knee, " any man is worth talking to—the poorest and most degraded has something to say. If he can't tell you how to live, he can tell you how *not* to live, and that's sometimes most important."

Leaning forward, he shaded his eyes to scan the horizon.

Johnny did not so much as wonder what he saw there. The sea was perfectly calm. Bits of seaweed floated here and there. A seagull skimmed low to drop like a single feather upon the water, then to rise and float away in the air.

Johnny's eyes lingered first upon the sea, then upon the girl, Madge Kennedy, who sat close beside him. He thought he had never known a finer girl. Brave and strong, good color, clear eyes, a clearer skin, strong as a man, yet tender hearted and kind, giving her spare hours to her grandfather, yet alert and alive to every sport and joy of life, she seemed worthy of a place in a great drama or a book.

"That friend of ours," said Kennedy, resuming his seat, " he will come out of his hole sooner or later. Then he's going to talk. Who will he talk to? To an old man. That's me. Everyone talks to an old man if he has a chance. Did you ever notice that, Johnny?"

"No, I—"

"Fact, nevertheless. You watch. Natural enough, I guess. When a man gets old, he loses the burning desire he might have had to become rich·or famous. He gets to feeling that he's about done his bit, and that it would be nice and pleasant to sit beside the road and give the younger ones a little advice. Don't you ever forget that, Johnny. When an old man talks, you listen. It's just as I said, if he can't tell you how to live, he can tell you how not to live."

Again he paused to stare at the sky. Wetting a finger, he held it up to the air.

"Wind's changed," he muttered to himself.

"When he comes out," he went on as if he had been talking all the time, "when this exclusive sort of millionaire President of the Fruit Company talks, I'm not going to tell him I'm part owner of this cargo. And you

needn't either. That way he'll think me a
harmless old man with a fair young granddaughter, and he may tell me things we need
to know.

"Johnny!" he exclaimed, springing suddenly to his feet. " I think we better run
for it."

" Ru—run for it," Johnny stammered in
astonishment. " Run from what?"

" The storm."

"What storm? The sea's calm, smooth as
a floor."

" Can't you see? Can't you smell it?" The
old man sniffed the air. " But then, of course,
you wouldn't. Me, I've lived here on this sea
always. I know things in advance. We're
going to have a storm, a regular humdinger,
a mahogany splitter, and if we don't run, if
we can't convince the captain we ought to run,
I don't know what's to come of us."

" Look!" said Madge, springing up.
" There's a steamer. See the smoke. You
can make her out too."

Kennedy unslung his binoculars.

"That," he said after a moment of close scrutiny, "is the *Arion*. She's the Company's steamer that our Unwilling Guest was to sail on."

"He'll be all excited if he sees her," said Johnny.

"Little good it will do him," grumbled Kennedy. "We'll be far enough from the *Arion* by night."

He hurried away to impart his all but miraculous knowledge of the coming storm to the captain.

The sea was still calm, though here and there, racing away with the speed of the wind, like hurried messengers, dark ripples sped across its surface. It was then that the Unwilling Guest left his stateroom for the first time.

Perhaps he was so well accustomed to sea travel that he could guess that their course had been altered. However that may be, he went at once to the bridge. There, after studying the instruments for a moment, he turned an angry face toward the stocky skipper.

"What sort of course is this for New York," he stormed. "You are not headed for New York."

"Maybe not," said the skipper, unperturbed. "Storm's coming. We were due for the center of it. We're running."

"Running! And not a ripple!" The magnate's voice was full of scorn.

As for the sturdy captain, he knew the sea. The scorn of the millionaire meant nothing to him. Quite unperturbed, he paced the deck and watched the roll of the storm clouds that mounted higher and higher along the horizon.

At the bottom of the companionway the capitalist found Kennedy sitting placidly looking away at the sea. Like Captain Jorgensen, he had lived long. One storm more or less did not matter.

True to Kennedy's prophesy, the rich man sat down beside him and began to talk. Who can face a storm without a companion?

" Going to storm, the captain tells me."

" Yes," rumbled Kennedy. "Be a mighty tough one over there." He poked a thumb toward the west. " Over there where the *Arion* is travelling."

The other man started. " That's our ship."

" She didn't change her course. Kept straight on. Good ship, though. May weather it all right."

" Do you mean to say," the rich man squirmed uneasily in his chair, " that it will be as bad as that? "

" Might be—over there." Again Kennedy's thumb jerked.

The topic of a man's conversation is very frequently determined by his surroundings and by the events that are transpiring about him. Was it thought of the storm and what it might mean to him that directed this rich man's conversation, or was it a casual remark thrown out by the strange old man who sat beside him?

" See those two bits of seaweed out yonder,

tossing on the waves?" Kennedy drawled. "Well, supposing one was you and the other me, and there wasn't any ship. Supposing I had houses and banks and bonds and you were a plain ordinary seaman with nothing but a chest full of old clothes. Do you suppose I'd have any better chance with the sea than you? Sort of strange, isn't it, when you think about it? Makes you feel unimportant and, and futile, you might say."

For a long time the man who owned buildings and banks, bonds and many ships upon the sea did not answer. When he did speak the thoughts he gave utterance to might not seem to have been an answer, and then again they might have.

"Our times," he said in a tone he had not used before, low, well modulated, modest and slow, "are very strange. Men, many men, most men perhaps, have come to think of capital as a great monster that always crushes the weak.

"But is that true? Take this Central America. It is true that we, the Fruit Company, have a monopoly of the banana importing business. But what was Central America before we came? Where miles on miles of bananas grow there was wilderness. Where naked half-savage people hunted deer and wild pigs, or sucked the milk from cocoanuts, there now lives a happy, reasonably prosperous and contented people. Who changed it all? Did not the Fruit Company do it?"

"I suppose," he said after a moment, "that our young friend, this Johnny Thompson who has somehow stolen a march on us and gotten hold of a cargo of fruit, thinks he's a young hero, a benefactor to mankind. I wonder if he is right."

"I wonder," rumbled Kennedy.

Time had been when Kennedy would have engaged this rich man of the world in sharp debate. He was old now. He had learned the futility of debate. Besides, he was greatly interested in the approaching storm.

At midnight Johnny Thompson found himself wrapped in a blanket and lying upon a plank, endeavoring in vain to snatch a few winks of sleep.

He found himself now standing almost upright on his feet and now tilted in the other direction until his very pockets seemed about to turn wrongside out.

" Some storm ! " he muttered.

Canvas boomed above him. The seamen had stretched a canvas over the hatch to keep out the spray. He was lying on that part of the hatch that had not been uncovered. Having given up his stateroom to the Unwilling Guest, he had been obliged to take a bunk below. During such a storm as they were now weathering, the air below was not to be endured.

Unable to sleep, he allowed his mind to wander. Had they indeed missed the heart of the storm, or were they in it now? How was the storm to end? He thought of the black rolling waves, and shuddered.

" If we weather the storm safely, what then?

Will we come to dock safely in New York? Will we be able to sell our cargo? Or will we once more face defeat? And what of the *Arion?*"

Scrambling to his feet, he plunged off the hatch, rolled to the deck, got Icaught in a dash of foam, struggled to his feet, caught the spray in his face, outrode a wave that threatened to carry him overboard, then made a dash for the wireless room.

"Had—had any message from the *Arion?*" He struggled to gain his breath.

"About ten minutes ago," said the young wireless operator. "Here it is."

"Arion laboring hard," Johnny read.

"That all?"

"All but—Wait. Listen!"

He thrust a head set over the boy's ears. Then his face went white.

"*Arion* leaking amidship. Settling by the bow."

For ten minutes, with the ship leaping up and down beneath them, with the thud of waves shaking her from stem to stern, they waited.

" She's gone; the *Arion's* gone down ! " said the young wireless man at last, mopping his brow.

" Say ! " He started as if struck by a ball. " That pick up we made, that rich man was going on that boat, wasn't he ? "

" He didn't," said Johnny.

" He's in luck."

For a moment there was silence.

" I suppose you know," said Johnny, " that the Captain must be notified. We couldn't have helped them; too far away. Have to tell him. But our Unwilling Guest, no use telling him, not just yet. No use to disturb folks needlessly."

" No," said the young wireless man, " no use."

Then for a time they sat catching the crash of the storm and wondering what ship would be next.

CHAPTER XX

HAIL AND FAREWELL

Fifteen minutes more of an ominous silence which told plainer than words that the steamship *Arion* with all on board had gone to her final resting place at the bottom of the sea. The very thought of it made Johnny feel sick and faint. The shrill scream of wind in the rigging became to him the cries of those who called in vain for aid.

"Couldn't we reach them?" he asked the wireless man. "There might be some we could save."

"Not a chance." The wireless man shook his head gravely. "Two or three hundred miles away. If we tried it we'd more than likely go to the bottom. Besides, there are two other ships closer than ours. I caught their answer to the S. O. S. They can't do anything either. The *Arion's* gone. God rest their souls!"

"Give me your report," said Johnny. "I'll take it to the Captain. Got to get out of here." He was shaking like a leaf. As he shut his eyes he could see forms battling with the black waves.

"Here it is."

Taking the paper, Johnny threw the door open and shot from the cabin.

The cool damp air revived his spirits. The battle he fought in making the bridge over the slippery water-washed deck put the old fighting spirit into him.

"We'll make it," he told himself stoutly. "This ship won't go down. She's Norwegian built. Done by the sons of ancient Norsemen. Her every plank and beam is selected—flawless and strong."

The grizzled skipper received his message without comment. On such a night one expects anything.

Battling his way back to the main deck,

Johnny crept forward to the main cabin. There, he remembered, was a long mess table, a cushioned seat or two along the wall, and some chairs screwed down to the deck.

"Might get a bit of rest," he told himself, yawning.

As he threw the door open a great gust of wind caught him and sent him in with such force that he went sprawling on the floor.

Grumbling to himself, he struggled to his feet. What was his surprise then to find himself looking into the eyes of Madge Kennedy.

"I—I couldn't stand my stateroom all alone on such a night," she told him. "I hoped some one would be down here, so I came."

"I am glad you did," Johnny struggled to a place opposite her, then looked across the table at her.

"You're not used to storms at sea," he said, noting the weary expression on her face.

"Not this kind."

"Nor anyone else I guess. Don't worry. We'll weather it. We'll be in New York one of these days with our cargo. Then the sun will be shining on both sides of the street."

"Will it, Johnny?" A wistful look came into her eyes.

"Do you know, Johnny," she went on, "I've been thinking to-night of our orchard and our jungle. I dreamed a bad dream last night. Dreamed that we couldn't sell the fruit, couldn't go back to our orchard and our jungle because there was no money.

"That would be pretty bad, particularly for Grandfather. He's lived there since he was a very young man. He loves it and he loves his black Caribs.

"You know, Johnny," her eyes became suddenly dreamy, her voice mellow, "I've read in books how people who live in other lands love their homes, their stone castles and their thatched cottages, their apple orchards, their groves and their tiny clustered villages. All that sounds fine, but very far away. For we too came to love our homes in the tropical jungle. To see sunset redden behind the tops of the tangled jungle, to hear the night birds call, to see the shadow of palms lengthen and lengthen, then to feel the damp of evening kiss your cheeks. Oh yes, Johnny, there is a charm in our land. And to us it is home."

"You'll go home," said Johnny with suddenly renewed determination, " and you'll go with that ancient alligator-skin traveling bag of your grandfather's bursting with bales of money. Never fear."

Reassured by his words, the girl bent her head forward on the table and fell asleep.

As for Johnny, he did not sleep. He waited, watched and dreamed.

The motion of the ship was something tremendous. Now she rose high in air to strike square into a great world of water; and now, lifting, lifting, lifting, she appeared to start on a flying trip to the stars, only at last to put her prow down as gently as a child drops his foot on a pebbly shore.

"She's a grand old ship," he thought to himself.

These were not his only thoughts. He thought of the great, gray-whiskered man and his granddaughter sitting there before him, the man who had given much to humanity and asked little in return.

Then he thought of the other one, their Unwilling Guest. " Providence," he whispered suddenly. " Providence took a hand. If we had not picked him up; if he had sailed on the *Arion* he would now be at the bottom of the sea. Wonder what he will think of that?

" Providence," he mused, " and back of Providence, God. God must have some work for that man to do, some great good work."

Morning broke at last and with it the storm passed. The wind went down. The sun came out. The sea was a thousand mountain ranges rolled into one, and all tossing about, rising and falling, like a new-born world.

The sea calmed. Hazy clouds drifted along the horizon. The *North Star,* somewhat battered by the storm, but still a very seaworthy vessel, held steadily on her course.

The Unwilling Guest came on deck. He seemed weak and somewhat thoughtful. No one had whispered a word to him of the ship that had gone to her grave, but the very force of the storm, the thundering peril of it had been enough to make any man thoughtful. Still he asked no questions, ventured no remarks.

CHAPTER XXI

ON THE TRAIL OF THE PEARLS

The Captain of the *Torentia,* the ship on which Pant had secured passage in so strange a manner, was a wary old seadog. On first indication of storm he had put in behind one of those small islands that dot the seaboard, and had there lain in safety until the storm had passed. This does not mean, however, that there were no interesting occurrences on board that ship to be recorded. As yet Pant had no certain knowledge regarding that thread marked gunnysack and its rich contents of pearls. Until he had made a try for that he could not rest.

To get a look at the chicle stored there in the forward hold was not so simple a task as Pant had at first supposed it to be. To begin with, it was a long way down to it from the deck where the few passengers were allowed to promenade. No companionway or ladder led to it. When it was necessary to take the temperature of the space where the bananas were stored the simple expedient of lowering a thermometer by a string was resorted to.

"Have to go down there some way, I suppose," he told himself. "Hand over hand perhaps. Trouble is, I have no rope, and besides there is always some one hanging about."

It was a strange situation. He wanted very much to go down there and inspect the chicle, yet he had no legal right to do so.

"It's not as if I meant to do anything that's wrong," he told himself. "If I told them what I wanted, there's not a man on board but would help me, help me a lot too much. That's the trouble. I dare not trust them."

On the second day out, he discovered a loose rope coiled up close by the hatch. But all that day seamen were working or lolling about close to the hatch.

" Try it at night," he told himself. " Use a flashlight."

He did "try it at night." He met with little success. Scarcely had he lowered himself to the bottom and thrown on his electric torch, than the night watch threw a more powerful light upon him, then shouted down:

" What you doin'? Come up out of there! "

There was but one thing to be done—to come.

The boy found his knees shaking as he climbed the rope. He had a wholesome fear of ship's discipline. On the high seas a captain is a king. What would be done with him now?

To his great surprise, nothing was done. The night watch took the affair as a boyish prank, and after a short lecture, let him go. That, however, ended his attempts to examine the chicle at sea.

" Have to wait until the stuff is in the warehouse," he told himself. " It will take some quick moves after that. I'll have to see some one high up in the Central Chicle office and get permission to make the search. Shouldn't wonder if I'll have to tell some one the whole story. Might be safe enough. Suppose it would."

After these settled conclusions he gave himself over to enjoyment of wonders of the ship and the changing mysteries of the sea.

So, freed from the grip of the storm, the two steamers smoked away toward a common port, New York. On board each was a somewhat worried boy, worried but eager; worried about the outcome of their adventure, eager for its end. The *Torentia,* being a faster boat, docked first.

Fortune was with Pant for once. Scarcely had the ship docked when he went springing down the gangplank. The doctor had looked at his tongue, the immigration official glanced over his papers, then set him free.

To find the offices of the Central Chicle Company he discovered was something of a task. Once there he found himself confronted by a long room full of clicking typewriters and a smiling but determined girl at the telephone switchboard.

" Mr. Daniels," he was informed, " is in conference.   Will   you   wait?   Have   you   an appointment? "

He, of course, had none.

" ' Fraid you won't be able to see him today."   The telephone girl threw back her bobbed hair.   " He goes out for golf at four."

"Golf! " exclaimed Pant.   " Tell him I must see him."

" I'll tell him.   But I'm afraid it's no use."

Mopping the perspiration from his brow, the boy sat down.   A half hour passed; three-quarters.   A buzzer sounded on the telephone girl's desk.   She hurried back to a mahogany walled office at the back of the room.   A moment later she reappeared, carried a sheaf of papers to a typist, then returned to her post. Not once did she glance at Pant.

" Forgotten me," was his mental comment. " That's the President's office she went into.

In the jungle we don't wait for things. We go after them. I'm off!"

With a quick elastic step, he cleared the low gate, and before a score of pairs of startled eyes, marched straight for the mahogany walled office.

" What's this?" a large, red cheeked man sprang to his feet as he entered. Two others at a table looked up enquiringly. " Who sent you?"

" No one sent me. I came."

" What for?" The man's face showed nothing. Pant felt uncomfortable.

" Chic—why, I—my grandfather shipped some chicle."

" Chicle. Go to the adjusting bureau. Can't you see I'm in conference?" The man's voice rose.

" But—you don't understand. You—I—" Pant was becoming more and more confused.

" Understand? Of course I understand. You want an adjustment on chicle. Can't you go where I tell you to?"

The boy was about to give up hope when a familiar voice from behind spoke his name.

" Why Pant, old chap! How did you get up here? " the voice said.

Turning, he found himself staring into the eyes of Kirk, his boy pal of that first adventure in the Maya cave.

" Is this some young friend of yours? " The man at the desk asked, turning to Kirk. His tone had suddenly grown warm and friendly.

" Why yes, Uncle, a very good friend from Central America. We had some adventures together. Remember the Maya cave? This is Pant."

" Ah, Pant. Glad to meet you." The man put out a hand. " Tell you what, Pant, I'll turn you over to my nephew. He'll help you out. If there is anything he can't do, and I can, come around."

" Thanks, I—oh! " Pant choked up, flushed, then backed awkwardly out of the office. His mind was in a whirl. So that was it, his companion at the home of the old Don was a favored nephew of the main stockholder in the Central Chicle Company.

"And I told him once I thought the Company unscrupulous in its dealings with smaller holders," he thought to himself. "I may have been wrong. I only hope he has forgotten."

Kirk had forgotten or forgiven, for he treated the boy from Central America like a long lost brother. Hurrying him out of the noisy office, he led the way to a quiet little eating place. There, after ordering a savory lunch, he invited Pant to unburden his soul.

"Time to tell the whole story," Pant thought to himself.

"Kirk," he said suddenly, leaning far over the table, "you remember the story of the first Don's silver box of pearls?"

"Yes."

"I found it."

"You didn't!" The other boy stared, unbelieving.

"I did. Pearls and all."

"Wha—where it is?" stammered Kirk.

" In a chicle sack somewhere in the store-room of your uncle's company."

" It is? How did it come there? "

The meal was eaten in haste while Pant told his story.

Leaving the dessert for some future time, the rich boy seized Pant by the arm and dragged him out of the place.

" Come on! " he exclaimed. " We haven't a moment to lose. Chicle is scarce. Your shipment will be sent at once to the factory. There it will be unsacked and broken up. Here! Jump in! " He dragged his friend into a taxi.

" To the Trans-Atlantic Dock," he commanded the driver.

CHAPTER XXII

A STARTLING REVELATION

What of Johnny and his precious cargo?

As the days passed and land, the shore of his native land, was sighted, the face of the Unwilling Guest once more took on a shrewd, calculating expression of a business man whose financial interests are vast. Already, in his mind, he was entering his office, was sitting at his desk, dictating letters, pushing buttons, issuing orders, calculating profits; he was sitting in financial conferences with other rich and successful men. Little wonder that his chest began to bulge as he strolled the deck.

They were not a day out from New York when Johnny Thompson decided to find out a few things. In spite of himself he had been worried beyond endurance with the thought that after all they had gone through they might be defeated in the end, that the powerful organization which was the Fruit Company would make it impossible to sell their fruit, perhaps even to land it.

" It is all right about the bananas," he said to Madge. " I can sell them direct to the pushcart men. Like to do it, too," he chuckled. " Be great to go down in the Ghetto and see the grinning faces of dirty little urchins as they devour cheap bananas."

" Grapefruit is different." His brow wrinkled. " Grapefruit must be sold to commission men. That's where they may have us. Commission men may fear the Fruit Company too much to buy from us."

" I'll get off a wireless or two," he told himself.

As he emerged from the wireless room a deep frown was on his brow. His worst fears had been confirmed. Barney Tower, an old trusted friend, had wired him that without the permission of the Fruit Company's President the Commission men would not dare purchase his cargo.

Johnny smiled a little grimly at thought of that very man, the President, who held all the power, being his Unwilling Guest.

"It's a queer situation," he told himself. "By the aid of Providence we saved his life. And yet, I would not dare ask him to lift the ban on our cargo. I don't believe it would be any use. The interests of his precious Fruit Company must be preserved at all costs. That's how he thinks of it, at any rate."

He sat down to think. Two minutes later he sprang to his feet.

"We might do it!" He raced away in search of Kennedy.

"Kennedy," he said, "you are a Britisher. Do you know anyone in Canada?"

"Why yes, I ought to. Yes, yes, I do. The harbor master in Toronto is an old war pal of mine."

"The harbor master. What luck! Kennedy, will the fruit keep an extra day?"

"Yes, Johnny, easily. Been cool air all the way. Storm brought it."

"Then we're safe. We're headed for Canada right now. Nothing can stop us. We'll sell our cargo there, and no one to bother us."

"But how about him, your Unwilling Guest?"

"We won't charge him anything extra," Johnny chuckled. "He'll get a lot of good out of the trip, find the sea breeze up there quite bracing." He was away on the double quick to notify the captain on the bridge.

Johnny was not the only one to note the sudden swing of the ship as she entered on her new course. The Unwilling Guest saw it and came storming down the deck.

"What does this mean?" he demanded angrily. "Changing course again? Another storm coming. Running again!" His tone was deeply scornful. "A day late, and running from a cloudless sky!"

"Not running. Just going somewhere,"

said Johnny quietly. " Just going on our way. Going to Canada."

" Canada! You said New York."

" Changed our plans."

" And how about my plans? Your plans!" The man's face was red. He stuttered in his rage. " Your plans! Your business! Floating a walnut shell in a teapot!"

" Pretty good old shell," said Johnny, glancing up and down the deck.

" This ship!" said the magnate. " Slow and clumsy. A very derelict! The *Arion* now, she's docked long since. If I had made Belize in time—"

" Wait," said Johnny. A new, compelling light was in his eye. " You wait. Come this way. I'll show you where you would have been."

Scarcely knowing why he did it, the rich man followed the boy to the captain's cabin where the ship's log was kept.

Turning back the pages, Johnny found the

record of that terrible night of storm. There, pasted in, was the wireless man's record.

" Read that," Johnny's voice was solemn.

As the man read, his face took on a deadly pallor.

" My God!" he murmured. " Can that be true? "

" All quite true," said Johnny huskily. " Had you not been becalmed out there in the Caribbean Sea, had you made Belize on time to catch the *Arion,* your Executive Council would now be in session. They would be electing a man to fill your place."

" They may be doing that now. Who knows that I am safe? "

" We do. No one else."

The rich man shot out of the cabin and away to the wireless cabin.

" Don't know that I should have kept it from him so long," Johnny thought. " But a shock now and then does us all good. It takes considerable of a shock to register with such a man."

That the shock had indeed registered, he guessed rightly enough as he saw the short, stout man, a half hour later, pacing the deck. With hands behind his back and head bent far forward, he appeared deep in thought.

Suddenly something seemed to come over him. His head snapped up. He spun around, then walked straight to the side of Johnny Thompson.

"Why did you change your plans? Why are you headed for Canada?" he asked.

"You should know the reason."

"Afraid of the Fruit Company's embargo? You need not be. I am the Fruit Company. I—why, I'll buy the cargo, buy it just as it stands right here in the Atlantic."

"You mean it?" Johnny's face was a study.

"Bring your papers to my cabin, and I'll show you, young man—"

A strange thing happened. The voice of the master business man, the head of a great corporation, broke and for a moment he could not speak.

" Young man," he began again, "I've been a fool."

" I'll go tell the captain to alter his course," said Johnny.

" There's one other favor I wish to ask." Johnny was seated in the Unwilling Guest's cabin. Perhaps by this time he might have been called a " willing guest."

" What is that, Johnny? "

" It's like this," said Johnny. " I hope I can make you understand. It must be wonderful to develop a business on a large scale, to see it grow and grow and grow, as you have been able to do. To add one ship after another, one plantation, one narrow-gauge railroad after another until the ships are a fleet, railroads a system and the plantations a little world all their own. I've dreamed of living such a life myself. It's a grand and glorious dream.

" But sometimes," his tone was slow and thoughtful, " it's hard on the little fellow.

Sometimes the great promoter, dreaming his great dream, forgets the little fellow, the man with a few acres of bananas, a few cocoanuts or grapefruit trees.

" The elephant enjoys himself as he goes thrashing his way through the jungle. But what of the small creatures he tramples beneath his feet? What about the butterflies he crushes with his swinging trunk? The butterflies appear to enjoy life as they flit in the sunshine. What of them? "

" Young man," said the magnate rather sharply, " come down to brass tacks. What is it you are talking about? "

" Well then, specifically," Johnny smiled broadly, " there is a fine old man named Kennedy who has a niece quite as fine. They live in a Central American jungle. Every Carib loves them because they love the Caribs.

" Until you signed this agreement they were very poor. The grapefruit aboard this ship is theirs."

" Not our Kennedy."

" Our Kennedy."

" Kennedy," the rich man mused. " That name sounds familiar. Can it be that a Spaniard name Diaz tried to purchase his grapefruit orchard for me? "

" Could be, and is true! " exclaimed Johnny, " That was the wily Spaniard's game, preying upon Kennedy's poverty. Planning to make a large profit off land he hoped to buy from a needy man for a song."

" Why did Kennedy not tell me? " the rich man demanded.

" Too modest, perhaps. And perhaps—you will pardon me—perhaps he thought it would do no good.

" Now," Johnny continued, " you are the Fruit Company. You said that yourself. And the Fruit Company refused to market Kennedy's grapefruit because one year he sold to an independent market. That's why they are poor."

" And now? " There was a strange look on the man's face.

"Now I want you to sign a contract to handle their fruit, a five year contract."

"Make it ten!" exclaimed the rich man, springing to his feet. "Have the purser write it up and bring it to me at once. I'll sign it."

"And by the way," he said as Johnny prepared to go, "have Captain Jorgensen come down when he finds time. This is a pretty good old ship, a mighty good one. I want her in my service. Give his owners a two years' contract. Or, I'll buy her straight out. She's the ship that saved my life. Along with two stubborn old men and a boy, she did it. You don't meet a combination like that every day."

The Unwilling Guest put 'out a hand to grip the boy's own.

CHAPTER XXIII

TREASURE AT LAST

With the aid of a flashlight Pant and Kirk were exploring a vast warehouse filled with sacks of chicle. They arrived in their taxi and having been admitted, had been told in a general way where they would find the last cargo that had arrived.

"Here! Here it is!" exclaimed Pant at last. "I can recognize the weave of my grandfather's sacks."

"Perhaps," he said after a considerable search for his particular sack, "the thread has been accidentally drawn out and lost."

"If it has," panted Kirk, "we'll open up every one. We—"

"There! There it is!" Pant pounced upon a sack. The green thread shone along its side.

With trembling fingers he cut the cord that bound it. A moment later, carrying a mysterious package wrapped in palm leaves, the two boys passed out of the door.

A second taxi was hailed. "We'd better go back to Uncle's office," said Kirk. "He—he's awfully square, and knows a lot. He'll tell us what to do."

Pant scarcely heard him as he was crowded once more into a taxi. His mind was in wild commotion. At last he was in New York, in possession of a vast treasure. Whose treasure was it, the old Don's or his own? He had read George Elliott's Romola, remembered Tito, the traitor to an old man, and recalled his terrible end.

"I will not be a traitor," he told himself. "If the treasure appears to belong to the old Don he shall have it, every penny!" At that his troubled mind found rest.

"I suppose," said Kirk, "that you have wondered how I came to be at the old Don's."

"Often," said Pant.

"Well, you see, my Uncle is my guardian. He holds nearly half the stock of his Company in my name. When I am of age it will be mine to manage. My Uncle believes I should know all there is to be known about the business, from the jungle to the wrapper," he laughed.

"So he sent me down there. He got the Carib giant for my bodyguard, and told me to go where I chose, only to keep my eyes open. I came at last to the old Don's. I liked it so much up there that I stayed a long time."

"Glorious, wasn't it!" said Pant. "I'd like to live there with the old Don for a whole year.

"This," he said, patting the package beside him, "will make the old Don rich."

"The old Don! It's yours!" Kirk stared.

"It's his by direct inheritance."

"How do you know that? Is there a monogram or a coat of arms on the box?"

"No."

"Then you will never be sure." The

younger boy's tone was earnest, entreating. "'Don't spoil the old Don by making him rich."

" It's not for us to decide what a man's rightful possessions will do for him," said Pant thoughtfully. " The only question for us to ask is, 'Are they his?'"

" Perhaps," he said after a moment's silence, " your Uncle can help us out."

" I am sure he can," said Kirk.

Nothing could exceed the astonishment of the chicle magnate when, having lifted the lid of the ancient silver box, his eyes fell upon the treasure of pearls within. Instinctively, he stepped back and locked the door to his office.

" That's the greatest treasure that ever rested on my desk," he whispered. " We must get them to the vault for the night. And you say they belong to Kirk's friend, the old Don?"

" I will tell you," said Pant. Sitting on the edge of a chair, leaning far forward, muscles tense, eyes aglow, he told the story of the beaten silver box from beginning to end.

"Well," sighed the magnate when the tale was told. "That's quite a yarn. Wouldn't believe a word of it if it weren't for this." He touched the silver box.

"Legally, in a court of law," he said, rubbing his forehead thoughtfully, "your old Don wouldn't have much chance. You could hold the pearls. Anyway, in this case possession is nine points of the law. You have only to pay the duty on them, then sell them."

"But I don't want—"

"You want to do the square thing," the magnate interrupted. "Then why not call it a case of salvage, and split the proceeds fifty-fifty. That will give each of you more money than you are likely to have any use for, and certainly more than you need.

"If your grandfather is interested in chicle," he added, "tell him I'll sell you an interest in our Company. Then in years to come you and Kirk will be partners. Pant and Kirk,

Chicle Exporters. How does that sound?"
He threw back his head and laughed.

"Great! Wonderful!" they exclaimed together.

The beaten silver box took one more ride
that day—to the Custom's offices. There it
was placed in a vault until the value of the
pearls could be settled upon.

A few days later the pearls were parcelled
out in groups and sold to several dealers for
a considerable fortune.

A few days after the docking of the *North
Star,* a happy group sat about a table in a small
dining room of the most sumptuous of New
York hotels. They had met there, Johnny,
Pant, Kennedy and Madge, for a farewell
feast. Business had been disposed of, and the
Kennedys were going home.

"Johnny," said Kennedy as he rose to stand
before a pretty open fireplace, "it would be
nice if we might have a bit of a wood fire.
Makes a fellow feel sort of cheerful."

"Not there. You couldn't," said Johnny.

" That's not a real fireplace.   It has no flue."

" Then what is it for? "

" To add a suggestion of comfort."

Only half satisfied, the old jungle man sat down.

" Seems a bit stuffy," he said a moment later.   " Let's open a window."

" Those are not windows," said Johnny. " They are looking-glasses that seem windows. We are probably a half block from any outer wall.   This hotel covers an entire block."

" A sham! " said Kennedy, rising.   " This whole thing's sham.   This is my party.   I'm paying the bill.   There's a real ship with a real cabin down in the harbor.   There are real windows in her that look, out on a real harbor. I propose that we eat there."

So aboard the ship they dined and talked. The food was good.   The talk was better.   Old days and new were discussed.   Pant was to sail with the Kennedys.   He was going back to Central America to make his grandfather and the old Don comfortable for life.   The

Kennedys were going home. That was quite enough for them.

Johnny, who alone was to remain, felt a little lonesome.

"Some day," Johnny said to Madge as they parted, "when I am tired, when the rush and push that is our America gets too much for me, I am coming back to Stann Creek, to listen to the thrum of the banjo and the Caribs' song, to watch the moon rise over the jungle and to smell the forbidden fruit ripening on the trees."

"Please do," said Madge Kennedy, brushing at her eyes.

"The latchstring's out and the door swings in," said Kennedy, gripping his hand, "and may God bless you for all you have done." So they parted.

Pant returned to the jungle. There he was destined to remain for many a day to come; for was not his Grandfather there and the old Don, and last but not least, the beautiful Senorita Ramocita Salazar? What better company could he ask and what more thrilling adventures could be found than awaits one at every turn of jungle trail.?

As for Johnny, the city with its imitation fireplaces, its mirror windows and much more that is artificial and unreal, could not hold him long. One day he met a curious sort of chap with a strange hobby. Fascinated by this man's tale of adventure, he joined company with him. The story of these fresh adventures in a land far from tropical wilds will be found in our next book, "Johnny Long-Bow."

www.ingramcontent.com/pod-product-compliance
Lightning Source LLC
Chambersburg PA
CBHW030239200626
46816CB00002BA/426